My Father,
the Nutcase

My Father,
the Nutcase

Judith Caseley

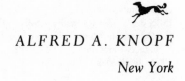

ALFRED A. KNOPF

New York

THIS IS A BORZOI BOOK PUBLISHED BY ALFRED A. KNOPF, INC.

Manufactured in the United States of America
10 9 8 7 6 5 4 3 2 1

Library of Congress Cataloging-in-Publication Data
Caseley, Judith. My father, the nutcase / by Judith Caseley
p. cm.
Summary: When her father becomes clinically depressed,
fifteen-year-old Zoe worries that his illness will engulf the
entire family.
ISBN 0-679-83394-3 (trade)   ISBN 0-679-93394-8 (lib. bdg.)
[1. Depression, Mental—Fiction.   2. Family life—Fiction.
3. Fathers—Fiction.]   I. Title.   PZ7.C2677Myf
1992   [Fic]—dc20   91-46750

To SUSAN MUNZ

My Father,
the Nutcase

one

My mother had bought the country-kitchen table with the pretty inlaid tiles under duress. Cara and I begged and pleaded and generally wore her down right there in the store, until, with a dazed look on her face, she handed her charge card to the salesgirl. My father was laughing. When we got him to load the table into the station wagon, instead of waiting for it to be delivered, he called us witches. We scrunched down happily in the back seat, with the box wedged against us. We didn't care. It was gorgeous. Then we gathered in the kitchen to give my father moral support as he put the table together. He squinted at the directions and said, "All this gobbledegook for a board and four legs?" It was amazing. A master's degree in business, and he's grunting and groaning, until finally the table is together and standing and Cara dubs it the leaning table of Pisa, and he has to do it all over again.

We've regretted it ever since. Every night after dinner, one of us has to clean between the tiles with a toothpick, a toothbrush, and a bowl of soapy water. So I'm scrubbing while my sister Cara washes the supper dishes. We're regular Cinderellas, while Rachel, our prima-donna sister, is reading upstairs. We squawk to my father, but he says something about Rachel doing a book report. I say the baby in the family gets all the breaks.

I grumble to Cara that it's grossing me out, digging in the cracks for poppy seeds and gravy and coffee-cake crumbs, but she doesn't answer. When I look up, I see that Cara has flipped her lid. One minute she's splashing around in the sink, and the next she's holding a spoon high up in the air and pretending to write on the window.

"Watch," she says, scribbling vigorously in the air. "What do you see?"

"I see that you've finally lost your mind," I tell her as she continues writing.

"I mean it," says Cara. "Watch my rear end. Am I jiggling?"

I gaze expectantly at her rear end, but it is still and calm, and I'm a little disappointed. What do I expect? It's smaller than mine, even though she's almost two years older.

"No movement," I tell her. I keep my jealousy to myself.

"Good," says Cara, squirting some liquid soap into a dirty pot on top of the stove. "I have to prove a theorem in front of the class tomorrow, and Mrs. Sutphin jiggles like crazy."

"So?" Suddenly I see the light—math class, Monday, Cara's crush sitting in the second row, the football hero she's mooned over for a century, and God forbid he should see an ounce of Cohen flesh jiggling in front of his face. "Ohhhh," I say knowingly. "Rambo again."

"Don't call him Rambo," she says huffily. "Billy is in the honors class."

"Brains and beauty?" I say, turning my back and writing in the air with my toothbrush. "Check me out, please. You never know."

Cara obliges, and my mother walks in and stands in amazement as Cara stares at my behind intently while I wave the toothbrush in the air.

"Jell-O," Cara says.

"Jell-O?" I screech. "That bad?"

My mother doesn't get it, because she says, "I thought you girls didn't like Jell-O. Rachel's the only one who likes Jell-O, and your father only likes it with bananas in it." Cara starts screaming with laughter, while I pull my hair out of my head, and my mother says, "What did I say? If you want dessert, there's some ice cream in the freezer."

I crane my neck to see if I can catch a glimpse of my rear end jiggling, and Cara says, "Hard Jell-O," like that makes it better. "You know. Not real loose, not like the kind that's hardly set."

"Oh, great," I say glumly, plopping into my chair and scrubbing once more at some disgusting piece of crud in the gorgeous country table we forced my mother to buy.

My mother gets it. She starts to laugh. "Bodies again?" she says with a roll of her eyes. "You're beautiful, both of you."

"Who's beautiful?" says my father as he walks into the kitchen. It's beginning to feel like a Marx Brothers picture.

"The girls," my mother says as she puts an arm around each of us. We resist like you're supposed to when your parents get goofy, but my father joins the circle, and I can still remember that picture, a scene from a family movie, as my father kisses the top of my head and then Cara's and then my mother's, one at a time.

And you can't even do your homework on the table. With all those tiles, it's too bumpy.

If Cara sounds a little crazy, she's not. I think she's the sanest one in the family, next to my mother. You know what they say about the oldest child: they get bossy and responsible, from being the first one to go to school, get pimples, get punished, and all that character-building stuff. And the parents get to make all their mistakes on them, and then they kind of ease up on the second one. Forget the third one— she's the princess, or the prince, like my cousin Edward, who sits around the house like a king while his sisters wait on him.

Anyway, when Cara told me there was something the matter with Dad, I believed her.

"What's the matter with him?" I asked her. "Is he sick?"

"Just watch him," she said to me.

So I watched. He went to work, he came home, he ate supper, he sat in the easy chair by the African violets and read his books. But there *was* something funny about him. He was different.

I told Cara I'd play detective, by taking a walk with him before dinner. My mother got a little hot and bothered. "Who's going to help me make supper?" she said, and Cara volunteered. It was a real labor of love for her, because when we left, Cara was shaping wormy-looking turkey meat into burgers, and Cara hates getting her hands dirty.

We started walking at a leisurely pace. My father lumbers when he walks, like he plans on getting there but wants to take his time. Mom always yells at him, "Hurry up, you're worse than the children!" and he looks surprised and quickens his step. But then he sees some stranger with a dog, and he has to stop and ask, "Is that a corgi?" Or he tells some lady in her garden, "Your hydrangeas are beautiful." The lady gets all pink and happy, and Mom walks on ahead with us, Cara and Rachel and me, muttering under her breath, "He's always charming the women," but we kind of know she isn't mad.

Only now it looks like he doesn't plan on getting there at all. I'm leading him down the street like we're walking down the hall of some nursing home and he's one of the oldest inmates. Forget the plant and tree identification, which used to drive me crazy. And when we pass old Mrs. Johnson on her knees in the garden, he doesn't even nod.

During supper, when Cara makes one of her jokes, Dad doesn't laugh. He kind of startles, the way the cat jumps when the doorbell rings, and then he realizes that everyone else is laughing, and he tries to laugh too. But it isn't a real laugh, it's some foreign strain. Last year, they taught us breathing exercises in school, relaxation techniques so we wouldn't crack up or anything. Breathe in from the belly, not from the throat, they told us. Dad used to laugh from the belly. Now it comes out of his throat, kind of forced, like it hurts him.

Cara is talking about her favorite subject, Billy the jock. She has won him, like a trophy, in less than a month, by *not* jiggling in front of the class. She's so smart. She wore her shortest skirt, and her best friend, Susan, told her that she was all legs, and no one could possibly notice her butt jiggling. Anyway, swift as lightning, Billy asks her out, and Cara is chattering away at the kitchen table, saying that the only thing she doesn't like is his macho car; it's so noisy when they drive through town that she feels like giving him a muffler for his birthday. Dad doesn't make a sound. He doesn't imitate Rocky or Clint Eastwood or pound on his chest like Tarzan. His pupils don't flicker. His face is stone.

"How's work?" I ask him, which isn't really something I ask my dad. I don't even understand what a systems analyst does. And usually my parents are so busy asking us about school and stuff, and we're so busy half-telling them, that we don't ask them anything. I mean, I know they're human. But it's two separate worlds, isn't it? So I ask him how work is, and his eyes are slow to focus, like he's coming back from the twilight zone. "Okay," he says, and he's tapping his fork against the side of the plate until my mother puts her hand on his wrist, very gently, and he stops.

That's when I gave Cara the "eyebeam." I caught her eye and she knew exactly what I was thinking. In the summer, if I come out of the water with snot hanging from my nose, Cara gives me the eyebeam and wipes her nose, very discreetly. Then I go under the water and take care of it. Who wants some cute lifeguard looking at you with something awful hanging from . . . Who am I kidding? The boys look at Cara—she's the vivacious one.

So Cara gave me the eyebeam back, and she knew that I knew that she was right about Dad.

My father left the kitchen and settled in his chair, and I started feeling a small glimmer of hope. Maybe if he picked up his book, and took out his worn leather bookmark, and plucked a few dead leaves from the plant next to his chair, and deposited them in the ashtray: maybe if he did all these ordinary things, he would miraculously recover. He would come back to earth, doors flipping open like in *Star Trek*, and we would have our real father with us again. The one who pretended he was Superman when we were young and watched the old *Superman* movies on television; only he would spread his arms and yell, "Stupid man!" I would get mad, but Cara would laugh hysterically, and they'd go zooming around the room trailing imaginary capes, laughing like hyenas, and collapsing on the couch, muttering, "It's a bird, it's a plane." By that time I'd be feeling kind of left out, thinking that my father loved her more than me. Then Mom would arrive and say, "Break it up, you two; I just had that couch covered."

Maybe that's why I thought Cara could pull my father out of his slump, or bad mood, or whatever it was. If anyone could, it was Cara. She was the one who made him laugh. So when Cara came into the living room and sat next to me on the couch, I eyebeamed her and she eyebeamed back, and her eyebrow was raised, saying, What are we going to do about this?

"Is something the matter?" Cara's voice cut through the air and made me jump. My father didn't move, his eyes glued to the open book, staring, not scanning.

"Is everything okay?" she said. "Dad!"

I held my breath.

He looked up and moved the corners of his mouth ever so slightly. He was trying to smile. Suddenly I saw the headline: MAN TURNS INTO ZOMBIE OVERNIGHT, and I would have said it out loud, except this was my father, and he didn't seem to know how to smile anymore.

I was relieved when my mother walked in. She leaned over my father and said, "I'm having a tough time with Rachel's math homework. Want to give it a try?"

He made that awful face again, a herculean effort, and said, "I can't, Lillian," so quietly that I could barely hear him. My mother was furious. She glanced sideways at us and said, "You can't? What do you mean, you can't?"

"Just what I said."

"And I can't carry this family on my back," she said, and I pictured it, me hanging from her neck, with Cara sprawled across her shoulders and Rachel straddling her waist.

"Don't do this to me," hissed my mother in the voice that wished us away but there was nothing she could do about it.

Cara and I sat, side by side, twin Popsicles eyebeaming each other, until Cara decided to become my father's defender.

"Can't you see he's had a bad day?" she said.

My mother scrunched up her face. "So have I, Cara. I work, I shop, I cook, I help you girls with your homework. . . ." But Cara had succeeded. She had driven my mother away. We heard her climb the stairs, then footsteps on the floor above us, and the slam of a door.

Cara was relentless. "Dad?"

"It's all right," he said, but his face was so sad that I knew his mother and father and sisters and brothers had all died in one single plane crash. Unless it was something else.

"Did I do something to make you mad?" My room was clean, my homework was done, I wasn't monopolizing the phone. I silently intoned bad deeds and discarded them.

He shook his head and turned toward the African violets, petting the small leaves. "It has nothing to do with you." We were dismissed.

two

On Saturday morning, I committed a crime. Unfortunately, I didn't know it was a crime until Cara came running into my room, screaming, "I hate your guts!"

"Don't pop your cork," I told her coolly, even though my stomach was doing flip-flops because I knew exactly what she was upset about.

I had been rummaging around in her desk for a bobby pin, and there it was. Cara's diary. So pink and shiny and enticing, sitting in her drawer like something out of *Alice in Wonderland* that said EAT ME. Only this diary said: "Read me, immediately, before you've even had your breakfast bagel."

So I read the final entry: "Today, Billy French-kissed me for the first time." I gasped out loud and kept reading. In the beginning, Cara didn't like it. But then she compared it to eating an avocado: you have to get used to the taste. It grossed me out, but I wanted to know more. Like what does Billy's tongue do in the mouth, exactly? I mean, does it lick the pizza off your teeth? Or does it dart in and out, like one of those tiny fish in the dentist's fish tank? I'm fifteen years old, but I'm sheltered. Of course I go to the movies, the ones with parental guidance suggested. I see all the kissing, I hear all the moaning and groaning, I see the sweat glistening. But it isn't real to me. Not like Billy Tommasino sticking his tongue in Cara's mouth.

After my reading session, courtesy of Cara Cohen, I went back to my bedroom. I made passionate faces in the mirror above my bureau. I looked like a moron, so I stopped and called up my best friend, Angie, and told her about Billy French-kissing Cara.

"So?" Angie acts like Tom Cruise is in the bed next to her and she doesn't need to know another thing. She yawns.

"What do you mean, so?" I'm indignant. And I'm beginning to feel like I'm the only one grossed out by some boy's fat tongue entering the privacy of my mouth. Four years of braces in preparation for that? Nurses learn to give needles by practicing on oranges. Too bad I can't drill a hole in one and make believe it's Alex Silvano's mouth. Orange juice is so much more appealing than saliva.

I had just decided that I was a naive fifteen-year-old when Cara burst into the room. Then I became a naive fifteen-year-old thief, traitor, and spy, all in one morning. How was I to know that she was a female James Bond and had wound a piece of thread around the diary so that she could discover spies like me?

Cara really gave it to me. I felt like the lowest of the low. And by the time I ate a cruller *and* a bagel for breakfast and rushed off to the library, where I was supposed to meet Angie, I felt rotten to the core.

Angie was a changed person. She hugged me excitedly and pumped me for information about Cara and kissing.

"I thought you weren't interested."

"I was trying to be cool in front of Margot." Angie glanced over her shoulder.

"Margot was over? So early?"

"She says she never went home last night."

"Were her clothes wrinkled?" I fell into my detective mode.

"A mess. Like she was wrestling in them."

"So who's the latest?"

"Boy! Sherlock Cohen!" But Angie was the cat that swallowed the canary. "Guess."

"Don't tell me Alex. Please don't tell me Alex."

"Jimmy." Angie had lowered her voice. "He's right behind us."

"Then according to the domino theory . . ."

"Alex is next."

I'm resting my head on the table, when Alex Silvano walks in, looking like he owns the library. Angie prods me, but I'm already alert and sneaking a look in the mirror stuck to my purse. We've been studying Greek gods in history class, and I can't wait until we get to the Romans. Alex is Italian.

He glances in our direction and works his way over to Jimmy Martin, who hoots at him until the librarian spears him with a long "Shhhhh!" Jimmy is cute too, but he's no Roman god.

"So finish telling me what happened between Margot and Jimmy," I whispered to Angie.

"According to Margot, he licked her all over."

"They were naked?"

"Clothes on, but he managed somehow, in the back of his brother's car."

"I'm sick. What is she, an ice cream cone?"

I'm also indignant, but I know what my mother would say. Something Shakespeare said, about protesting too much. You know, if you get mad enough, it really means you want it. Except I'm afraid I'll never want it.

"Maybe if Margot is going with Jimmy, you'll get to see more of Alex."

Even though she's whispering, I dig an elbow into her ribs. I get a whiff of cologne and wonder if it's Alex's. Once I bumped into Alex after gym class, and even his BO smelled good. That's when I knew I was hooked.

I muster up some bravado. "So what flavor is Margot today—vanilla, chocolate, or butter pecan?"

"Chocolate chip. She has a few zits."

We burst out laughing, and the librarian gives us the evil eye. We're chastened.

"We're just as pretty as she is," I whisper. "She's just more . . ."

"Aggressive? Witty? Is it her C cup?" Angie tickles me with a strand of blond hair. My father says Angie and I complement each other, and I guess we do. Her pale honey blondness and my cool darkness, or something like that. But both of us have breast envy. She's even smaller than I am, which means she's practically concave, because I look as if I'll be wearing a training bra the rest of my life.

I heard Margot come into the library before I saw her.

"The book was trash anyway," she announced. "You're better off without it."

"You still owe us five ninety-five," said the librarian, real poker-faced.

"Would you take a check?"

Margot is like that. Maybe I'm slow or something, but I don't even have a checking account. I get my allowance from Dad, put it in my pocket, and it's gone the next day. Margot wrote out a check and gave it to the librarian, who held it up to the light. If it was a gold coin, she would have bitten it.

"Do you believe these people?" I smell Margot's Opium, the perfume Mom uses for special occasions. "The book is rubbish, and they make me pay for it anyway." She threw her jacket on the chair next to mine and swung her head dangerously down between her legs, shaking her hair. Then she straightened up and ran her hands through the tangles. She patted me on the head like a puppy dog and sat down with an enormous sigh. I couldn't help liking her again.

Margot picked up a book, read the last page, and discarded it. "I see the Pillsbury Doughboys are here," she said. I had no idea that she had seen them. Sometimes, when I'm feeling shaky, I try to conjure up Margot's nonchalance. She's a pro at looking like she doesn't care.

She lowered her voice. "Did Angie tell you about Jimmy and me?"

"A little," I said. That's the funny thing about Margot. She's an open book. And she doesn't mind being gossiped about. Whatever you don't know, she'll tell you.

"Jimmy's all right," said Margot. "He's hot."

I thought I caught some hesitation in her voice, like she was going into a descending scale. She drummed her fingers on the table.

"I'm still a virgin," she said, matter-of-factly. "Just chalk one up for experience."

"You mean it won't be long now," said Angie, laughing.

Margot shrugged. "Who can tell?" She stood up and jutted her hips to the side, not looking behind her once. There was no doubt about it, her hips were a little large, but I took no comfort from that. The rest of her was full and rounded and . . . womanly. No one would ever call me that.

Margot waited, and I started to feel like I was watching a play. Jimmy called her, right on cue. She walked over to him and whispered something in his ear. He laughed, and I heard him say, "It beats studying." Then she walked back to our table and gathered up her coat and stuff. "See you guys," she said, and she headed out the door. I heard a chair behind me scrape, and there was Jimmy, beating a hasty exit. End of Act I.

Angie and I looked at each other.

"Does she give lessons?" I said.

"Do we want them?"

I knew what Angie meant. I mean, there are fast girls and popular girls, and then there are the fast popular girls. Angie and I sort of fall between the cracks.

A few minutes later, before I could look in the encyclopedias near Alex, Volume C or something, he left.

I figure I need more than lessons.

"The rotten son of a bitch!"

I walked into the kitchen and flinched at the words, immediately guilty.

Rita Whiteman sat at the table, her head buried in her hands.

My mother gave me an embarrassed look and said, "Rita's visiting," as if I didn't know.

Rita shifted in her seat and said in a weak voice, "Oh, Zoe, sweetheart." She wiped her eyes with the sleeve of her sweater.

Rita is my mother's oldest friend. Whenever they're together, they gossip and giggle and generally make fools of themselves. I don't mind Rita. She made a big fuss over me when my braces came off and gave me the free trial lipstick you get with the purchase of perfume by some fancy company.

Rita is usually a worn kind of pretty-looking. Today, she is a wreck. Her eyes have raccoon rings, and her nose is red. "She's twenty-four years old," Rita said. "A dental hygienist." She took a deep breath, and it came shuddering out. "He runs off with the bimbo who cleans his teeth."

I'm beginning to get the picture now. I don't like it. Adults are supposed to have it all together. Maturity comes with age and all that. So how come Bert Whiteman, who has black hairs growing out of his nose, ran off with his dental hygienist? I can see her picking away at his plaque with those awful hooks, and old Bert, who must be at least fifty, raising his bushy eyebrows in appreciation. And she *must* have seen the hairs in his nose from that angle. She must have.

My mother placed a steaming cup of tea in front of Rita, and Rita bent low over it, blowing on it and shaking her head. She looked like a nutty old lady.

My mother sipped her tea too, straight-backed. Her mouth was a thin line, and I wanted to tell Rita, "Look, we have problems of our own," and a picture of my dad, the walking, talking space cadet, came to my eyes. But Rita was sobbing now, and my mother's hand patted her like a mechanical doll. I felt sorry for both of them.

As I left the kitchen, Rita raised her head and between sobs said, "Zoe, Zoe. I'm so sorry you had to see me this way." Then she looked at me with her watery raccoon eyes.

I told her not to worry about it, and I went upstairs.

"Thank you, Zoe, sweetheart," she called after me.

Rita Whiteman is actually responsible for my name, which is truly terrible. When I was born, Rita gave my mother a present. Everyone else brought presents for the baby, but Rita said my mother deserved one for playing classical music every night to her belly and for eighteen hours of labor. "She was a trouper," my father told everybody, and my mother said, "He's just thankful I didn't scream nonstop like the lady next to me." Rita always said that the worst pain she ever experienced was getting a bikini wax. Anyway, she gave my mother this perfume called Zoe, and that was it. My mother changed my name from Callie to Zoe. I think it's weird being named after a little bottle in a box. But Callie Cohen would have been no better. A Jewish Daisy Mae or something. I was born embarrassed.

I can't say that I'm surprised about Rita and Bert. It's not that Rita is an awful person. Bert is the awful one. I remember one day at a picnic, I handed him a plate of pickles, and he said in a weird voice, "Is that a pickle in your pocket, or are you glad to see me?" My father said, "Don't be an ass, Bert," and Bert had this fake surprised look on his face. He held out the pickle plate to my father and said, "Look, Ben, remind you of anyone?"

Rita said swiftly, "Hand me a gherkin, and I'll tell you who it reminds me of," and Bert dumped the plate of pickles in the garbage can. Just like that.

I honestly didn't know what they were talking about. A year later, when I was thirteen, I found out. We were sharing a house in Cape Cod with family friends, the Kolnars. Frankie Kolnar was a tall and very gawky fifteen-year-old, who didn't say a word to Cara or me for the entire month. He grunted in the morning, went out for the day on his bicycle, and returned to the privacy of his room in the late afternoon. Nobody knew where he went, but he left every morning like clockwork.

One morning, Frankie's mother told me I could go into his room and borrow a book. So I walked in without knocking. I had a heart attack on the spot. There was Frankie, gazing admiringly in the mirror and holding the biggest hot dog I had ever seen. Only it was attached to his body. He turned and screamed at me, and his mother came running and my mother came running and I burst out of his room and ran into the only room in the house with a lock—the bathroom. I locked myself in. My mother stood outside and hissed, "What happened? What made him scream that way?"

"He didn't have any books," I told her.

So that was sex to me. A plate of pickles and a hot dog.

three

By Sunday morning, Cara was talking to me again. Breakfast was a strained affair, with my father pushing food around on his plate and my mother finishing her coffee at the sink.

"Eat something, Ben; you're losing too much weight," she said. After that, she didn't utter a single word. Cara rolled her eyes at me, and that's when I knew I was forgiven. We ate our bagels quickly and went up to her room.

"I've hidden it," said Cara.

"Hidden what?" I answered, all innocence.

"The diary. And if you tell a single soul about it, I'll kill you."

"I promise." I was glad she had taken temptation away. I know it's sick, but I'd read it again. It was like I was searching for something, some truth about boys and kissing and sex and whatever my sister thought about life. Maybe she'd even write about me. Once, in the bathroom stall at school, I overheard someone talking about me. First I wanted to disappear, and then I leaned forward and tried to catch every rotten word, until a toilet flushed and they were gone. So I was glad Cara hid the diary.

I watched my sister examine her face in the mirror. She has my dark eyes and dark eyebrows, but on Cara everything is more petite. Dad says Cara has a delicate beauty and I'm striking. Frankly, I think the word sucks. I mean, you strike a match, you strike a person, you go on strike. Do any of those make you feel good, make you feel beautiful? No way.

"So do you like it?" I asked Cara.

"Like what?" Cara took the cover off her lip brush and dipped it into a pot of gloss.

"Frenching." I got right to the point.

Cara raised one dark eyebrow. I can't do that. "Of course," she said, applying a coat of shiny rose to her lips. "You should try it," she added.

"Don't you think I would if I could?" I said, wondering how my own sister could be so stupid.

She waved a lip brush at me. "I mean, you should try a lip brush, dope. And don't blot. That only smears the color."

When I was little, I remember standing in the bathroom and watching my mother put on her bright-red lipstick. It was a serious business. She would lean into the mirror and part her red lips. Then she'd take a tissue and blot her lips carefully, dropping the tissue into the wastebasket. Mom raised the roof when she found a drawerful of red-imprinted tissues in my room. Dozens of them. Pretty little paintings that I wanted to save.

I took out my honey gloss stick and swiped some across my lips in my usual manner, mirrorless. Blend with index finger across lower lip. Blot. Voilà. "The Zoe School of Makeup," I said, smacking my lips.

"Fast-food fashion," said Cara smugly. "It takes a little time to look natural."

I felt like using my index finger on her, a small swipe at her perfect rosy mouth, a swift imprint on her nose. I didn't want a lesson in makeup from her; I wanted a lesson in life. But there was a knock on the door, and Rachel was whining to come in.

"Come," Cara shouted.

Rachel walked in as I held my leg right under Cara's nose and said, "Look how natural I am. Check out my hairy legs."

Cara snarled, "Get your leg out of my face before I puke."

"Mine are hairy too," said Rachel.

"Blond hairs don't count," I told her.

"How come?" she said, but that's Rachel, all innocence. I mean, she hasn't even gotten her period yet. I rolled my eyes at Cara.

Cara changed the subject. "Dad looks terrible. Billy thinks he should see a doctor."

"Billy?" I snorted. "Billy? What does he know?"

"What's the matter with Dad?" said Rachel, but Cara talked over her and told me that Billy was going to major in psychology when he went away to college.

"You mean a college took him?"

"Syracuse, if you want to know."

"You've got to be kidding. And they give courses in jock-strap psychology?" I don't know why I went in for the kill. Zeroed in, pressed the button, and waited for the rockets to explode.

"You are such an asshole!" Cara shouted, right on cue. Her eyes were flashing now. "Just because he's a football player, you think he has no brain."

"I think he's cute," said Rachel.

"He's a jerk," I said flatly. I turned away. Maybe if I got mad at Cara, maybe if I filled the room with a crackling bang-up fight, I could forget about my father.

I faced her again and fired a last round. "He has the brain of a yo-yo," I said in the voice my mother uses that I hate the most.

Cara hasn't lived with me fifteen years for nothing. She was silent for a moment. Then she said, "What, Zoe?" just like that.

So I told her. "Dad."

"What about Dad?" said Rachel.

"There's something the matter with him," said Cara. "We'll talk to Mom."

"Mom will know," I said to Rachel. But I wasn't convinced.

On Monday morning, I put on my best black pants and my longest red sweater. I brushed my hair until it was shiny and glinty like the coat of our Irish setter before he died. I applied my makeup carefully, Cara-style. I gave myself the once-over. Feel pretty, I willed myself. My sweater covered the part of me that made me hate to leave a room, all eyes glued to my backside. The sweater draped gracefully. I looked . . . curvaceous. I breathed deeply, smiled coquettishly into the mirror. Confidence, I whispered. Today I would talk to Alex Silvano.

Alex had other ideas. I could see him, bent over his locker, as I fiddled with my combination. He slammed the door shut and smashed a fist into the metal. "Shit!" he said, turning sharply. He was coming my way.

My voice squeaked hideously, Pee-wee Herman instead of Kathleen Turner. "What's the matter, Alex? Can I help?" I sounded just like my mother.

Alex jerked his head. "I left my goddamned sneakers at home. Buckley is going to kill me."

"I've got size-nine Nikes," I said weakly.

"Give me a break."

English class was small comfort. Mr. Shapiro was talking about *The Waste Land*, and I suddenly understood certain passages. It was about my life. I like English, even though part of me fights it because of my mother. She teaches English at Uniondale College, and if she had her way, I'd be reading every waking moment. Mr. Shapiro praised me: "First-rate, Zoe," and my pulse raced a little with the pleasure of it, until I remembered about Alex.

At lunchtime, I rewarded myself with a bag of chocolate-chip cookies. "Take that," I said, smacking a hip and making Angie spit out her sandwich, laughing.

"You'll be sorry!" she sang. She eyed the bag of cookies and waited patiently.

"All right, all right," I said, and I smashed the bag, grinding the remaining cookies into crumbs. Habit. If I'd been at home, I would have sprinkled some scouring powder in with the crumbs, just to make sure I wouldn't weaken and go foraging.

"Hey," protested Angie, "you could have offered me one first."

"You're my conscience," I told her. "You don't deserve to eat."

"You're lucky you have me." Angie softened a little. "You look good today, Zoe."

"Really?" I was glad she said it. I can get up in the morning, early, to fix my hair just right and put on my natural makeup, à la Cara. I can wear my great sweater. I can think I look good. But I have to hear someone say it, so that I can really truly believe it. I guess that's Zoe Cohen's definition of

low self-esteem: when you think you look good but you re-
fuse to believe it until someone else tells you. Sick.

"Move over." A tray crashed into mine and pushed it to
the other side of the table. Margot sat next to me and moved
me along the bench with her hips.

"So?" She sounded like my grandmother, waiting for the
latest gossip.

"Nothing new," I said. Margot wouldn't tell me I looked
good. It wasn't her style. "How's Jimmy?"

Margot unwrapped an ice cream cone and took a long lick,
like she was in a television commercial, with the wet red lips
and the creamy white ice cream. Except on TV the model's
eating yogurt and she's real skinny. Then she runs her tongue
over her lips and looks like she's about to make out with her
boyfriend, not eat yogurt.

"Jimmy's an ass," said Margot. "I just saw him in the hall,
very chummy with Lynn."

Margot was real casual. I would have died on the spot.
She concentrated on her ice cream, sucked some from a hole
in the point of her cone.

Angie leaned forward, eyes wide. "Did you say anything to
him?"

"Let's just say I made my presence known."

"Jimmy's a jerk," I told her. "And you have a much better
figure than Lynn Baker."

"Shake-it-and-bake-it Lynn?" Margot shrugged. "I thought
Alex had the hots for her."

My heart froze. Angie shot me a look and said, "How
come?"

"I saw them at Grumpy John's a couple of nights ago."

I could have ripped my sweater into shreds. Maybe sabo-
taged my diet and bought an ice cream. Instead I took out
my pen and slid over, pretending to work on my English

assignment. I doodled a circle and cut it into a pie, blackened every other wedge. Then I couldn't resist, I just couldn't, and I scribbled a heart and, inside, Z.C. *loves* A.S., then I added an *S* to Alex's initials and blackened the whole thing so thoroughly that no one could ever read it.

The rest of the day was a washout. I dragged myself through algebra and only perked up in choir, because it was the last period of the day and Alex sang in the back row. I'm a glutton for punishment.

On the way out, I slowed down to a snail's pace, waiting for him to pass me so I could catch a glimpse, even if it was the back of his head. Then he was next to me, and he threw me a sidelong glance. "Hey," he said.

My heart froze for the second time.

"Hasn't anyone told you?" he said.

My heart was beating furiously now. "Told me what?" I said. That I was beautiful? That he loved me?

"That you have ink all over your face."

"No," I said. "Nobody told me."

"Check it out," he said, and he was gone.

four

Angie got analytical on the way home. "He noticed ink on your face, right?"

"Right. Like a two-year-old kid."

Angie shook her head. "Wrong."

"What do you mean, wrong?" I swiped at a bush for emphasis.

Angie was patient with me. "He sits way behind you in choir, right?"

I swiped at the bush again.

"You didn't have any other classes with him today, did you?"

"No. So?"

"So how did he notice that your face had ink on it? He must have been looking at you."

"You've lost me," I told Angie.

"He looks at you," Angie said. "He likes you." Angie turned the corner and yelled, "See if I'm right!"

"You're crazy!" I called after her as I crossed the street, but I tucked Angie's little nugget away in my head. I figure there's kind of a jewelry box in there, for keeping all the good stuff.

A police car was parked outside the house when I got home. My mind was working overtime as I pushed open the front door. I stood frozen in the hallway. I could hear voices above me. Police in my bedroom? Had I made my bed? I pictured my mother slumped over my mussed-up blankets. Headline: MOTHER DEAD OF HEART ATTACK FROM DAUGHTER'S UNMADE BED. And underneath it: "Zoe Cohen said she meant to make it, three days running, but whined why should she when she just has to get back into it at night?"

I mounted the stairs slowly, and suddenly my mother was alive and well. I could hear her voice rising above the rest, and she sounded very healthy, because she was asking someone to please not lean his head against the wall. It was just painted.

"Hello, young lady," said a blue-uniformed officer, smiling as he passed me on the steps. He was young and cute. And he wouldn't smile at me if disaster had struck, would he?

My mother, white-faced, came into the hallway from her bedroom.

"Everything's all right," she said quickly.

I know it's sick, but the minute I had her reassurance, I tried to figure out if I was too young to date a policeman.

"Your father had a car accident, a small one. He's resting."

"Why are the police here?"

"They brought him home. He wouldn't let them take him to a hospital."

I started for the bedroom door, and my mother held up her hand like a stop sign. "Don't be scared when you see his face. He cut his forehead. Dr. Meggs is coming."

Cut his forehead? It occurred to me that maybe, like in some old movie when the amnesiac cracks his head, my father would benefit from his accident. He would come to his senses miraculously. I pushed open the bedroom door.

His eyes told me otherwise.

The gash didn't bother me. It really didn't. I'd seen worse in the movies, much worse. *Night of the Living Dead* had it all over my dad's gashed forehead. Actually, there was a connection. His eyes were the eyes of a dead man. I remembered Angie's grandfather, stretched out in his coffin, pink-lidded and pink-cheeked. Except Dad's eyes were wide open.

He tried to smile. "I had a little encounter with a tree," he said, his voice without inflection.

"Back to nature is one thing, Dad. But this is getting ridiculous." I stood a foot away from the bed. Maybe I could just tell him to snap out of it, let's talk about cute policemen and whether or not I should go out with one, and what would people say if I was dating a cop? A strand of hair fell across his eyes, and I tried to will myself to get closer and smooth it away. I didn't move.

Cara burst into the room. "What happened?" she said, and she swept past me and perched next to my father and pushed the hair away from his eyes. Just like that. I felt like some tiny country with a newly elected government, green and unsteady as the tanks arrived and flattened me. Combat Cara. She always acts on her feelings. I always feel them, they sear me with their heat, they burn up my insides, but they stay inside my body.

I think my mother is a little like that, even though she's an adult. I went downstairs, and there she was, sitting on the couch smoking a cigarette. I was mesmerized by it, trembling on the edge of her lower lip.

"Since when do you smoke?" I said accusingly.

"I smoke in emergencies," my mother replied, her voice level.

"How did it happen?" I tried not to whine.

"He ran into a tree. I can't really tell you any more than that." She took a drag on the cigarette, looked at it with distaste, and stubbed it out in the ashtray we keep on the coffee table for company. "It doesn't help," she said into the air.

"So long," said my cute policeman, standing in the doorway with a clipboard in his hand.

My mother stood up. "Thanks so much," she called to him.

He smiled past her at me, and I smiled back at him, and I had the weirdest feeling, like I was mad at my father because I couldn't just smile at a policeman. Instead I had to worry about him upstairs in his dark bedroom with his dead eyes, and I said to my mother, my voice rising, "So what happened? You don't just drive into a tree! Was he avoiding a cat or something?"

My mother fixed her eyes on me, suddenly aware that I was a short-fused firecracker.

"He drove into a tree, honey. Just like that." Her voice trembled a little.

"On purpose?" I shot the words out of a cannon.

My mother's face shook as if she'd been hit. She was reprieved by the doorbell.

"Dr. Meggs," she said, and she went to let him into the house, all calm authority as he followed my mother up the stairs.

"Why isn't he at the hospital?" I heard him say.

"He wouldn't go, John. The paramedics said he was acting like a crazy man. He kept shouting, 'I want to go home.' "

A crazy man. My mother's words chilled me. I knew that my father's moodiness was more than just getting up on the wrong side of the bed. It wasn't just a bad week at the office. My father was crazy. A nutcase.

The car accident was the ominous beginning. In the next few days, there was a lot of muffled talk behind closed doors and whispered phone conversations with Dr. Meggs. The house felt haunted by my father, cloistered in his room, and by my mother, shadowing him.

She told different stories to different people. It was alarming. She had this high-pitched he's-just-got-a-cold voice when anyone from work called. Urgency when it was the doctor.

This time it was Grandma Rose. We could tell by the easy, natural tone. My mother washed dishes while she talked, knowing that Grandma wouldn't be insulted by the sound of running water and clanking cutlery.

Cara and I sat in the dining room, eavesdropping, if you could call it that. Mom knew we were there. Maybe it was the coward's way out. She still couldn't break it to us in person. So we heard it from the next room.

"He quit his job."

Cara and I widened our eyes like cartoon characters tied to a railroad track, watching the approaching train.

My mother continued torturing us. "Just what I said. God knows what we're going to do for money." She clanked a frying pan. "The mortgage payments." Clank clank. "Rachel needs braces."

She told Grandma everything. They say that knowledge is power, or something like that. I say bullshit. Ignorance is bliss, believe me.

"And what about Cara's college tuition?" The water was going down the drain now; I could hear the gurgling.

Cara stiffened, and I put my hand out to stop her from fleeing. She pushed me away. "Don't leave," I whispered.

Cara perched on the very edge of the dining room chair like one of those big birds—a heron?—about to take off.

Rachel's bus screeched in front of the house, and she rang

the doorbell insistently. I let her in, and she hurried past me, throwing her coat on the couch and her books on the table.

"Hang up your coat," I told her in my mother's voice.

"Later," she said, unmoved. "I'm starving."

I followed her into the kitchen. If Rachel could go, fearlessly, so could I. "Hi, Mom," she said, as she rummaged through the cabinet for a box of cookies. Mom always says that Rachel nibbled her way through childhood. My mother despaired. "She was a bundle of bones. She would only eat bananas." Rachel is not a bit like me. Frankly, I think anyone who doesn't think about food all the time is downright lucky. A package of Oreo cookies? No problem. She'd eat one, maybe two, and be satisfied.

Rachel ate a cookie now, humming. It never occurred to her that we were seated in our cozy kitchen, in our cozy house, smack in the middle of a tornado. I envied her.

At least our presence stopped the onslaught of my mother's revelations. She busied herself with a can of scouring powder, her head tilted to support the phone. "Yes, Rachel just got home. Do you have any homework, sweetheart? Grandma says to tell you she loves you."

I munched on my third Oreo cookie, and my mother, eyes in the back of her head, snatched the bag away from me. "You'll spoil your appetite," she said.

Big deal. My life was already spoiled.

five

Billy came over after supper. Cara
was pretty used to him by now. She didn't get so crazy about
what to wear and whether her hair was okay and if the pim-
ple on her left ear showed.

We went up to the bedroom and closed the door. The
three of us. Cara never let me stay with her and Billy. Billy
was her private property. But this evening was different. We
were going to talk to Billy the jock psychiatrist about our
father, the nutcase.

"He quit his job."

"He what?" Billy grunted as he pushed off first one sneaker
and then the other. "Sorry, guys," he said, waving a hand
through the air. "Basketball practice."

Cara wrinkled her nose. "We heard my mother tell my
grandma," she said to him, taking a container of Lilac tal-
cum powder off her dresser and sprinkling some onto his
feet.

"Hey!" said Billy, springing up from the bed. "Do you
want me smelling like a wuss or something?" Cara giggled

and shook more powder on him, and Billy did his macho thing, kind of wrestling with her, and I completely lost it and started shouting at them that it wasn't funny.

Lately, it seems like everything gets me mad. But Cara put down the powder and Billy settled back on the bed, resting his head against a poster of Bruce Springsteen.

"Sorry," he said, clearing his throat. "From what Cara tells me, your father's in deep trouble."

"No kidding," I said.

"He's in crisis," said Billy, ignoring my sarcasm.

I was slightly impressed. In crisis. It sounded vaguely authentic. But you could say that about Cara when she got a huge blackhead, or about me when I gained a few pounds.

Billy took out a pocket-sized spiral notebook, the jock reporter now. "Let's talk symptoms," he said. He consulted the pad. "Does he have an appetite?"

"No," said Cara, watching me to see if I was sufficiently impressed.

"Does he talk much? I mean, does he initiate conversation?"

"No. He's a brick wall," I said.

Billy jotted something down. "Listless. No appetite," he said out loud. "He's an early riser, isn't he?"

"Not anymore," said Cara. "He used to get up at five-thirty, putter around, make breakfast."

"He used to race-walk, for God's sake." My voice sounded unnaturally loud.

"Slow race-walking," Cara added. "Then he'd get on the train and go to work."

"He was full of energy." By now I was focusing on Billy like he was Dr. Freud, alive and well.

"And now?" Billy readied his pen.

Cara dropped her voice from soprano to alto. "He stays in bed."

"All day?"

"Most of the day. Mom makes him come down for dinner. Sometimes he gets out of bed and vacuums."

"Vacuums?"

"Mom leaves him a note in the morning, a list of chores."

I leaned forward expectantly, waiting for Dr. Billy Tommasino's diagnosis.

Billy consulted his notebook, made some checks on the page, closed it, tucked it carefully away in his shirt pocket, put the cap on his pen, and cleared his throat.

"I'd say it's a case of severe depression," said Billy. "He's in deep trauma."

So was I. I don't know what I'd expected. I have eyes and ears. As for Billy, I had a new respect for him.

On Saturday morning, my mother confirmed it. After the chores were done, she called a family conference. She wasn't smoking, but I could smell her breath a mile away.

"You smell funny," said Rachel. Trust Rachel.

My mother laughed, an uneasy laugh, not the kind she gave when she watched an *I Love Lucy* rerun. "I just brushed my teeth, honey. I guess it didn't help."

I knew what she meant. Some days, when I'm nervous about a test or something, I feel like my breath stinks no matter what I do. Now I have a fear of bad breath—there must be a word for it, like agoraphobia—and I'm always covering my mouth and breathing at my hand to see if I can catch a whiff of something rotten.

My mother took a sourball from the glass canister next to her and unwrapped it.

"Your father is sick," she said quietly. "He quit his job." She twisted the plastic wrapper, rolled it into a tiny ball. "I don't want you children to worry. I have my job, and we'll just have to tighten our belts."

My mother looked very serious. She *is* very serious, being a college professor and everything. A month or two earlier, before Dad got sick, I went to a Saturday workshop with her. It was a real eye-opener. When she walked to the front of the class, my heart was beating wildly. Frankly, I was afraid she was going to make a fool of herself, or a fool of me. She started talking, and to my amazement, her students listened. They didn't throw spitballs, they didn't pass notes or crack wise. And my mother made jokes! As the class ended, she gestured toward me. "A very serious critic, my daughter, has been sitting in on this class. To see how well her mother teaches." The class laughed, and my mother widened her eyes, almost as if she was flirting. "I know it's hard to think of me as anything but a teacher," she said, laughing. "My daughter finds it hard to think of me as anything but a mother!" I smiled but stared straight ahead at the notes she had written on the blackboard about Romantic poets. Then she turned to me and said, "Was it too boring?" like it really mattered to her.

Sometimes it's hard when your mother becomes a real person and shows you her insecurity. I guess I have these preconceived notions—adults are never insecure, grandmothers are always good cooks, Jewish people never commit crimes. . . .

My mother was steely-eyed now, not a trace of insecurity. "There will be no excuses when it comes to Saturday-morning chores. I can't afford Mrs. Cooper anymore, so everyone will have to help me. That means ironing too." She smiled at Rachel. "I'll give you lessons, sweetie. We'll start with your gym shirt."

Rachel almost wagged her tail. She looked happy at the grown-up prospect. I knew better, although I certainly wouldn't miss Mrs. Cooper. Every Thursday, she came to clean, and every Thursday morning, my mother straightened up beforehand. I never hung around in the kitchen after school, in case she turned up. Sometimes I would bump into her coming out of the bathroom with her bucket and old rags. She'd fasten her beady eyes on me, and I'd know what she was thinking: A grown girl like you should be cleaning this filthy bathroom for your mother. Mostly, she stayed in the basement like a mole, ironing and washing clothes and even eating her lunch down there in front of the old black-and-white TV. No, I wouldn't miss beady-eyed Mrs. Cooper.

Rachel asked what everyone was thinking. "What's going to happen to Dad?"

"He's going to start seeing a psychiatrist," said my mother. "He'll get better," she said firmly.

I wanted to believe her, I really did. Rachel said, "What does a psychiatrist do?" and my mother stared blankly for a moment.

"He'll help your father," she said, and even though she was sitting in the sunlight, I thought a shadow crossed her face.

Rachel still wasn't satisfied. "How?" she said.

My mother took a deep breath. Cara and I leaned forward expectantly, as if the truth would finally come out.

"Your father is in a state of depression, girls. His mind isn't functioning." She paused. "Not the way it should be. It's . . . it's a disease."

"A disease?" I said. "What do you mean, a disease?" I

pictured an army of depression cells, roaming through my father's brain.

Rachel looked stricken. "Like cancer?" she said.

"Not exactly," said my mother. "But there could be a chemical imbalance in the brain. We just don't know."

"Will he really get better?" said Cara, taking up where Rachel left off, braver than I was.

"There are drugs the doctor could prescribe, called antidepressants. They might do the trick," said my mother hopefully.

"What if they don't?" said Rachel.

I knew I should shush Rachel. My mother was dangling on a hook, impaled and flopping.

"The doctor will talk to him," said my mother flatly. "Every week."

I couldn't understand it—a disease that took the form of sadness and emptiness, not bleeding or swelling or blotched skin or physical pain.

Rachel didn't know it, but she was utterly ruthless. "What will he talk about with the doctor?" she said.

"His family, the past." My mother was starting to sound desperate. "It's very complicated, Rachel!"

"He'll be fine," I said, rescuing my mother at last, but it was my heart that was on the hook now, impaled and flopping in uncharted waters.

s i x

When I was little, I found a poem my father wrote, tucked behind the metal cup of pennies in the top drawer of his dresser. Cara and I stole from it often, petty crime like five or ten cents. My father knew it. Reading the folded piece of paper was somehow different, much worse than stealing, like I was eavesdropping on my parents' conversation through their bedroom wall with a glass or something. I read it anyway.

> My madonna lies, flat-bellied and white-sheeted,
> Past roundness safely resting in the basket next to her.
> My beauties, my life, my wondrous
> Wife and daughter in a white room.

I knew it was about Cara, because it was dated before I was born. I remember wishing it was about wondrous and beautiful newborn me. With all my heart I wanted it to be me. I started writing poetry instead.

Even though my mother was an English teacher, I rarely showed her my poems. I kept that honor for my father and, as he read, waited impatiently to lap up any words of praise, like a hungry kitten. I'd scan my father's face, and when he pursed his lips and raised an eyebrow and said, "You should send this out for publication—it's wonderful, Zoe," my heart would swell. I'm not kidding.

Now that Dad is sick, I don't show him my poems anymore. He never asks, and I never offer.

Mr. Shapiro sort of took over. He made me assistant editor of the *Pen and Quill*, the school literary magazine. Part of my job is to recruit people to write. That's the hard part. It means I'm interested in more than boys and clothes and stuff. Sometimes I wish I was like my aunt Cindy. She's a housewife, and it's her chosen career. In the morning she does her housework, has lunch, starts dinner, putters in the garden, and watches "her shows." That's what she calls the soap operas. Then she gets dressed for dinner and waits for her husband to come home. She loves her life.

And me? Back before my father was sick, if I was home with the flu or something, I'd switch the soap operas on in secret, and if my father called in the middle of the day, I'd lower the sound real quick, so he couldn't hear. It's not that he'd yell or anything. It's just that I felt I had a reputation to uphold. I had to be literary. I'd much rather be flirting and worrying about my makeup. So now I worry about everything: Whether I seem like a "literary" nerd. Whether I'll ever find a boyfriend who likes me and my fifteen-year-old body. Whether I'll be a good kisser. Angie says I think too much. Maybe she's right.

At the last English class of that week when I learned my father was sick, Mr. Shapiro gave me a signal just before the bell rang. I stood up and gave my speech. "Anyone interested in submitting something for the *Pen and Quill*, our deadline is on the first of April. Just give me your work before then."

I sat down quickly, banging my knee on the desk. Ungraceful, uncool.

"It doesn't have to be poetry," Mr. Shapiro added. "And you can write about anything—love, war, the cafeteria. Try to keep it on the clean side."

"Hey, down and dirty is better, Mr. S." Jimmy shot a fist into the air, and the class laughed.

"So write about it, Jimmy, and I'll let you know."

"I already let him know," said Margot as the bell rang.

Mr. Shapiro didn't skip a beat. "Write about *that*, my girl."

I know why Mr. Shapiro said it didn't have to be poetry. Writing poetry is not cool. Angie knows about my poems, but she doesn't broadcast it. Though I don't want to come off like a dumbo with nothing upstairs, I don't want to threaten anyone, either. When Margot found out that I wrote poetry, she just gave me a look and said, "Weird." The deadline was approaching for me too, and this time, the entire high school would read what I wrote. I wanted it to be unusual—racy or cool or clever. Pretty flowers wouldn't do it.

Friday nights are definitely the best part of the week. Nobody does homework on a Friday night, not even the good students, like me. Two whole school-free days lie ahead, and tonight Angie and I have a mission. Or should I say *I* have a mission and Angie will tag along? Does Alex Silvano really have the hots for Lynn Baker? Sherlock Cohen will track him down and find out.

As I swing past the dinner table, Rachel rolls her eyes. It startles me, because it reminds me of Cara. "I wish *I* was getting out of here," she says in a low voice. My parents don't look up, but I'm looking at Rachel, who is stuffing her face now, and she seems different. I don't stop. I have to meet Angie.

We're having supper at Grumpy John's. That's John's Pizzeria, but nobody calls it by its right name. Grumpy John is the old man who makes the pizza, seven days a week as far as I can tell, from eleven in the morning until eleven at night, twelve on Saturday nights. He's always yelling at his wife in rapid-fire Italian, and the wife retaliates by yelling at the customers, who could easily be called a bunch of masochists if it wasn't the best pizza in town. You don't go there for good service or fancy decor. Six plastic tables covered by six plastic tablecloths, oversized jars of oregano and parmesan cheese, no napkins. You have to ask for napkins, and then the old bag glares at you and gives you one. Tonight, three of the tables have paper mats with maps of Italy on them, hastily thrown down whenever Mrs. Grumpy gets a chance.

Angie and I take the table in the corner, a fine lookout point. I have my back to the wall, which makes me feel more secure, or at least less uneasy.

Angie settles her coat behind her. "Pizza?" she says, rubbing her hands together. Angie isn't afraid to show how much she loves to eat. But since Angie is slender, she doesn't have to worry. Still, I'd rather have a friend who likes to eat than a friend who doesn't. I'd have to hide a whole part of myself.

"A medium pizza," I tell Mrs. Grumpy. We can stay longer if we order a whole pie. A single slice, and old one-napkin eagle-eyes will toss us out on our ears.

"Sody?" Sometimes Angie slips into this weird kind of baby talk, like "milky" if she wants a glass of milk, or "Wahhhh!" if she's upset about anything, but when you see her mother, it figures. She looks a little like an aging movie star, but the Bette Davis type, lips painted larger than her real mouth. She never calls Angie by her real name, which is not Angela. It's Angel, but Angie banned it from her mother's lips at the age of eight. It didn't matter, because Angie's mother calls her "babycakes," "sweetness," "princess," or "my petal," which is the very worst.

"Soda?" I bat my eyelashes at Angie. "Yes, my petal," I add, scooting out of the way before she can give me a kick. "I'll go tell the pleasant lady behind the counter."

The Grumpys are at it. I stand quietly as the old man mutters under his breath and slaps sausage on a pie like it's some rotten kid's behind. "That's not our pizza, is it?" I ask timidly. Mrs. Grumpy, grizzled hair flying, throws up her arms and screams, "Lady, that's not your pizza," so loud that my face flushes and tears spring to my eyes. Then I feel mad that the stupid old witch can make me cry. I return to our table.

"So where's the soda?" Angie says.

"You get it," I tell her. "That woman is a maniac."

Angie gives me a look and springs up, heading for the counter with her little rear end twitching like mine never will. I know it's only a matter of time before she finds a boyfriend. Maybe brains matter more than they used to; I don't know. But a good behind doesn't hurt.

Angie is leaning over the counter when Alex walks in, alone, looking like he owns the place. He glances around, and his eyes meet mine, and something begins to tremble. I think it's my knees.

The wild woman pulls a steaming pizza out of the oven. Ignoring Angie, she steps out from behind the counter and sets the pizza in front of me. Alex watches. I feel like I have a sign hanging around my neck: Miss Piggy. Oink, oink.

He says, "Hungry?" but he's smiling, and it makes me feel a little better. Angie zooms over to him. "Help us eat this pizza," she says, and Alex sits down opposite me. I'm a little jealous that Angie gets to slide in after him, but maybe it's better this way, because my knees are still shaking.

"You're right about her," says Angie, tipping her head toward the counter. "She's nuts. That marriage has driven her over the edge."

"Remind me never to get married," I say. Alex drums a number on the table.

A stream of Italian fills the room, and Alex laughs.

"She's telling him he's too generous with the mozzarella and that it's costing them a fortune."

"What's he saying?"

"Not for your ears, ladies."

"They'll be divorced by the time we get our soda." I wait for someone to take the first slice. I give the pizza an uninterested look.

"Maybe he'll murder her with the pizza cutter," says Angie.

"Hey, we're about to *eat* here," I say, hoping she'll take my cue.

Angie reaches for a piece. "Maybe it sounds worse in Italian. My parents fight all the time."

"At least it fills the silence," I say, instantly hoping I haven't revealed my tomb of a house.

Alex puts his hand up. "Listen," he says. "A new development." The wild woman is on the telephone now, gesturing excitedly as if the caller can see her.

"They're not getting a divorce," announces Alex.

"Well, they should," says Angie.

"They will never get divorced," he says smugly.

"How can you be so sure?" says Angie.

"Because that's her mother on the phone, and old Grumpy John is her father."

I watch them carefully now. The father shapes a lump of pizza dough, flattens it, and practically plays Frisbee with it. He ladles some sauce onto it. Then he takes a handful of mozzarella and glances swiftly at his daughter. She raises an eyebrow. He mutters something as he sprinkles the cheese over the sauce. She slaps her hands together, and a puff of flour is released into the air. Then she starts to laugh, and he joins her, red in the face and bending over his white-aproned belly.

I think of my father, and I feel nauseous. He never yells at me anymore; I don't exist. Too much television used to drive him crazy, or one of us forgetting to empty the dishwasher. One night before he got sick, he came upstairs and pulled me out of bed. Scared me to death, he looked so angry. "I want to make myself some tea," he said, "and there's not a cup on the shelf." He practically dragged me downstairs, and I emptied the dishwasher as noisily as possible. I hated him.

And now? It's a muddled kind of hatred, and I push it back, down into my gut, because how can you hate a sick man?

Alex gives Angie a slight shove. "Move over. I have to get out."

"Have some pizza," I say. "There's plenty."

"Thanks," he says. "I'm meeting someone."

I can't tell if there is any regret in his voice, because I've choked on a gulp of soda as Lynn Baker walks in. It would seem strange if I change seats with Angie now, so it's too late to spare myself the experience of watching Lynn and Alex make out at the corner table. Before their pizza even arrives. Before it's even ordered from Grumpy John's damned daughter.

I write a poem when I get home. It's funny how hatred and disgust get me going, instead of clouds and flowers and stuff like that. I can hear the muffled voices of my parents in their bedroom, mostly my mother talking. I write faster.

The darkness descended like snow
down the chimney
into the bedroom
onto the bed of the father,
who didn't blink
didn't brush the wetness
from his eyes
didn't sweep the cold
from his covers.
The father banked
the blackness around him,
pulled it to him like a friend,
embraced it gladly.
The father, black snowman, ice daddy,
didn't melt at the sight of his
daughter or wife
didn't weep at the sunset.
He died quietly.

I didn't kill him off. I don't wish him dead. I want him living and yelling and reading my poetry and making us scrambled eggs and bacon on the weekends and dragging us on awful hikes. It just doesn't look like it will happen. Billy's words pop into my head. In crisis. That's me.

seven

On Saturday morning, I agreed to go with my mother to Grandma Rose's. Cara was spending the day with Billy, as usual, and I kind of liked being the only grandchild. We dropped Rachel off at a birthday party. We took Dad with us. I know it sounds like Dad is some mindless kid, some three-year-old who gets led around. But he's still an adult to me—my father. I guess he's my missing-part adult. Like some portion of adulthood is gone from his brain.

My mother grunted as she drove, using her brake constantly. There was a steady stream of speeding drivers to the right of us, to the left of us, weaving around us. My mother gritted her teeth and made no eye contact, did no lip-reading. I was the one who read the lips: Asshole. Stupid bitch. Crazy woman driver. But my mother took the speed limit to heart. Fifty-five miles an hour. That and the middle lane were her lifeline.

My father used to do all the driving. Not anymore. He was on medication now, and he wasn't allowed. My mother always drove herself to college and back, but she was an uneasy driver, who took the side roads as often as she could. Highways spooked her. To get to my grandmother's, you had to take a highway. I think that's why she was grunting so much. My father sat beside her, staring straight ahead. There were none of the usual fights about which road to take because if you took the other one you could avoid the traffic at the racetrack. My father didn't say a word. So we got caught in traffic.

The cars in front of us came to a complete stop. My mother opened the window and stuck her head out the way truck-drivers sometimes do, except they're ten feet higher and maybe it helps. I think she was looking for some kind of accident, a bunch of rubberneckers. Anything but the racetrack. She hates racetracks. Even when they hold the flea market there and Angie can get us a ride. She wrinkles up her nose like there's a bad smell somewhere.

My mother switched on the radio. "Any requests?"

"Doesn't matter," I told her. I was beginning to feel carsick.

"Ben?"

My father shook his head and started to speak. His voice was hoarse. "I didn't hear what you said, Lillian."

"So what else is new?" She switched off the radio.

I held my breath in the back seat, willing her not to lose her uneasy control, willing myself not to vomit. The car stopped and started, my mother jamming the brake in a violent dance step.

"Fucking gamblers," she said.

She never swears. I could almost see her anger, stretched and swelling like some gigantic bubble.

"I wonder if Grandma will make rice pudding." My voice contained a plea, but what was I pleading for?

Traffic was moving, and my mother hit fifty-five again.

"She knows you're coming. I imagine she will. And chicken soup for Dad."

She stretched an arm along the back of the car seat and touched my father's head.

"What?" he said.

My mother drew her hand back quickly, stung by a rattlesnake. She didn't answer. We finished the ride in silence.

Grandma's kitchen was littered with dishes. A platter of roast chicken, a bowl of homemade coleslaw. ("No onion," she told me. "Your father gets heartburn.") A plate of blintzes, a pan of tsimmis, an old gefilte fish jar full of stewed fruit. I went straight to the refrigerator for ginger ale, which I poured into a jelly glass. All the staples were there: prune juice, eggs, butter, low-fat milk, whole milk, nondairy creamer—something for every diet. It was not a one-person refrigerator. Grandma cooked the same way she always had, for company. Grandpa had been dead for years, but there was always company, and no one ever went home empty-handed.

We carried the serving dishes to the dining room table, which was laid with plates and cutlery from various hotels, glasses inscribed "Chase Manhattan Bank." "One dollar at the temple auction," she announced. "A bargain."

"You're still not using the dishes I gave you?" My mother reminded her every time and expected the same answer. Grandma waved a hand at the mahogany and beveled-glass cabinet and said, "Sweetheart! They're for company!"

"And what are we?" My mother was softening; I could tell. Maybe Grandma would create a miracle and get her to laugh.

Grandma put her arms around my mother and planted a red imprint of lips on my mother's cheek. "Family, honey, you're family." Then she took the corner of her apron and dabbed at my mother's face.

It was my turn now, and I let Grandma hug me hard. "How's my favorite grandchild?" she said.

"You say that to all of us," I chided her.

"And I mean it every time." It was my father's turn, and she threw her arms around him, like he was her son and not just a son-in-law. She held him close and said, "My poor Ben," and when she drew away, I thought I saw a tear in my father's eye.

My father turned and found his way to the table. He rallied with "Rose! Where's my chicken soup!" in a voice faintly reminiscent of my grandfather's.

I caught my mother's look of surprise as she passed me on the way into the kitchen. "How many knaidlach?" she called out to him. Before he could answer, she emerged, in a slow kind of wedding march, the steaming bowl of soup her bouquet of flowers. She placed it in front of my father. "I gave you two," she said. "If my mother can't fatten you up, no one can." My father dipped his spoon immediately into the soup and ate hungrily.

I ate my two dumplings out of duty. I didn't have the heart to tell my grandmother that it was Rachel who loved knaidlach. Cara loved the stuffed cabbage. And I thought Grandma, who never baked but always had a bakery box of rugelach handy, made the creamiest rice pudding. I dug into my chicken, my coleslaw, my tsimmis, eager for the next course.

"So?" She eyed me now. "How's the poetry? When are you going to show me? My granddaughter the editor doesn't even show me her poetry."

"Assistant editor," I said. "You wouldn't like it."

"Let me be the judge of that," she said. "Who do you think you get your talent from? I got published in the senior-citizen paper."

"I wrote a poem last night," I said, casting a look at my father.

"So? Did you bring it?"

"It's too grim, Grandma."

"Aha." Grandma tore off a piece of roll and slathered it with butter. "Realism."

I laughed. "You might say that."

My mother cut in. "Is that butter you're eating? I brought you a twin-pack of margarine a week ago. You have to watch your cholesterol!"

"I don't have cholesterol. Just a little pressure, and I didn't put a drop of salt in the soup. The butter is unsalted, for God's sake." Grandma groaned as she pushed herself up from the table. "It's my arthritis that's killing me."

"What does the doctor say?"

"Bufferin." Grandma rolled her eyes to heaven. "And Florida, God help me. He said I need a warm climate."

"You could live near Aunt Sara. Maybe over spring break I could go down with you." My mother's voice faded as my grandmother shook her head vigorously. Grandma hooked a chin toward my father. "And leave Ben?"

My father was actually listening. "I'd manage," he said.

Grandma disappeared into the kitchen. "It's not for me," she called out. "Lilly, come and get some dishes for dessert." My grandmother rounded the corner carrying a casserole dish. My mother put four Hunter Hotel bowls on the table.

"I'm telling you, the card games would kill me. I'd die of boredom." Grandma spooned a mound of rice pudding into a bowl. "For you, darling," she said, handing it to me. "Besides, I like my job. My arthritis isn't so bad that I can't push the keys on a cash register."

"Mother, you can barely walk."

"I walk a block to the bus, I take it, it lets me off right in front of the store." My grandmother stood up. "Coffee," she said, and she left the room.

I ate silently, savoring the creamy rice, a gift from my grandmother, who remembered.

It was late afternoon when we left. My mother's face had lost its tightness. Her driving was calmer. She reached over and smoothed the hair on my father's sleeping head.

I woke at the slamming of the car door. My mother ran up the sidewalk and rang the doorbell of a house I didn't recognize. A bunch of balloons was tied to the mailbox, and I remembered Rachel's party. My sister appeared, and as they waved goodbye and headed for the car, it hit me like a ton of bricks. Rachel was getting fat.

eight

She wasn't obese, actually. But you couldn't call her a bundle of bones anymore, that's for sure. Maybe it was a sign that she was growing up. Maybe at twelve it's normal to start getting fat. Rachel, the baby of the family, was almost a teenager. I never heard her talk about boys or anything, unless she did it with her friends. I just knew I didn't want her to grow up and start worrying about pimples and boys and fat. And our father.

And dieting. At Sunday breakfast, she devoured four pancakes to my three. Cara had two, and my father had one. My mother had whole-wheat French toast fried in some low-cholesterol goop. She ate distractedly and shoveled two more pancakes onto Rachel's empty plate.

"She's had enough!" I said.

"Oh." My mother lifted the spatula. "How many have you had?"

"Four," said Rachel, digging her fork into a golden fifth.

"Rachel! You'll make yourself sick!"

Rachel shoved her plate away. Her face darkened, and she

scraped back on her chair. "Can't you all just leave me alone?" she cried.

It didn't sound like Rachel. It sounded like me. I'm the moody one, the one they called Bulldog because my mouth was always set in some kind of frown. Maybe getting grouchy was another initiation into adolescence.

After breakfast, my mother dragged us on a hike. Cara said, "No way—I'm meeting Billy," but my mother was adamant.

"Call him up and tell him you'll see him tomorrow."

I sat in the back seat, sandwiched between the gloom-and-doom sisters. I didn't dare talk to either of them. Rachel had her head glued to a paperback. I just hoped she wouldn't throw up five pancakes all over me. Cara picked a certain spot on the horizon and stared at it for thirty minutes. I began to feel more cheerful.

We pulled into a tree-lined street. The houses were disappearing, and it started looking like the countryside. My mother swung off the road and parked next to an old pickup truck. A small sign marked WATER TOWER pointed toward an expanse of woods.

"Not another shitty water tower," said Cara.

My mother shot her a withering look, and Cara said, "Oh joy, oh rapture, another water tower." Cara's nervy like that.

Rachel said, "I'll wait here."

My father opened the car door and stood patiently beside it, a dog ready to be taken for his walk. My mother banged a fist on the trunk as she ran around to close his open door.

Suddenly I was the good one, the only one who wanted to take a hike, my mother's ally. "Is it my imagination, or does the medicine make him even slower than usual?" I said to her conspiratorially.

My mother ignored me and stuck her head inside the car.

"Get out, Rachel," she said, in a controlled voice. Rachel didn't move.

"Get your butts out here, both of you! Now!" Cara scrambled out, and Rachel moved more slowly, milking her rebellion, turning the flame under my mother down to simmer.

My mother faced us. "Conference time," she said grimly.

We gathered together under a nearby tree. Rachel sat on a gnarled root, and I sat next to her. She was beginning to change before my very eyes, all sweetness gone, darkness descending. Cara perched near my father.

"We are a family," said my mother. She bent and picked up a dry branch from the ground. "I will not stand by and see *this* happen to our family." She pulled a brittle twig off the branch, then another, and another, until the branch was bare.

I was surprised by her dramatics. My mother continued: "We are hiking to the water tower. The long route. I won't stand for any grumbling. We are a family."

She sounded like one of those leaders in an old prisoner-of-war movie, with Richard Attenborough or someone, where one of them wants to make a daring escape and the sergeant says they all have to stick together.

"I'm cold," said Rachel, and the movie changed location to Mount Everest, where one of the climbers wants to stay behind, he can't walk another step, and the leader hauls him over his back and stumbles forward, stony-faced, resolute, blue-lipped.

"Start walking and you'll warm up," barked my mother, the sergeant, and the troops followed.

It wasn't too bad. My father surprised us all by spotting the first crocus. I felt a turning in my stomach, not from the pancakes, or the car ride, but from the change of season, with its suggestion that something, a sprout, a bit of green, would spring from my father.

We reached the base of the water tower, a huge metal cylinder with tiny claustrophobic steps spiraling into the blue sky. Rachel pulled a fast one, sat down on a rock, and said, "There's no way you're getting me up there."

My mother didn't argue with her. She started up the tower with a soft clanging noise as her sneakers touched each step. My father stumbled after her, slowly, unevenly. Cara followed, a surefooted mountain goat dancing her way up the trail.

I stood uncertainly next to Rachel, the stranger. "Do you want me to stay down here with you?" I asked.

Rachel shrugged. "You don't have to."

"I will if you want me to."

"My stomach hurts."

"Mom's whole-wheat pancakes," I said, not adding that she'd pigged out on them.

"I hate my life," said Rachel, and it hurt me to hear her, because she reminded me of me.

I didn't know what to say. I sat down next to her, put a hand on her shoulder. "It gets better," I said, not telling her that I hoped it would, that it had to, because right now, most of the time, life sucked.

Rachel leaned over her stomach, hugged her knees to her body, and rocked slowly.

"Do you want a wintergreen?" I said, fishing my hand into my jacket pocket.

She shook her head and continued rocking.

"Hello, down there!" I heard Cara call, and I leaned back and saw her waving from the top of the tower. I was glad that Rachel and I were at the bottom. It was too easy to picture hurling bodies landing with a thump on the ground in front of me. I watched for my father, fearful now, but soon I could hear the metal thump of footsteps. Cara first, then my mother and my father.

"What a beautiful view," said my mother. She fixed her eyes on us, her "little women," so far from Louisa May Alcott that you could puke. "Shall we head back down to the car?"

Rachel sat upright and pushed herself off the rock like an old man. She put her hands to the back of her pants and froze.

"Oh my God," said my mother.

The rock was dark with blood. The back of her pants was a crimson stain. "You got your period," I said lamely.

Tears welled up in Rachel's eyes. "I don't want to get my period," she said, and my mother put her arm around her and said, "You're earlier than I was," like Rachel really cared. My father stood watching, the outsider. Then he took off his jacket and pulled the white sweatshirt over his head. "Here," he said, handing it to Rachel. "Take it, sweetie."

Rachel looked bewildered. "But I'm not cold anymore, Daddy."

"Wrap it around you, honey, and we'll start back."

Cara sprang forward and tied it around Rachel's waist. "Nobody would even notice," she said.

Rachel looked at my father. "It will get dirty," she said, pulling on the arms of the sweatshirt.

"It doesn't matter," my father said gently.

"Do you have cramps?" my mother asked anxiously.

"It's awful," said Rachel.

"When we get home, I'll give you something for it." My mother started back down the path into the woods, and the family followed.

So maybe it was her period that made her say that she hated life. That makes sense, doesn't it?

nine

*E*arly on Monday morning, I could hear my mother talking through the wall. I pictured my father lying in bed, the covers pulled up to his chin. My mother was putting on her bra—no lace, slightly padded—pulling a plain half-slip up around her hips, full hips like mine, and God forbid her body should show through her skirt in a blast of sunlight. Then her merino wool skirt with three small pleats, that I wouldn't be caught dead in. And a pin on the collar of her shirt, nothing trendy, maybe a butterfly or an agate wrapped in silver. And the shirt would be cotton, because the material had to breathe, right? And presto! She was an English professor. Then she would hang up her nightgown and robe, tell my father, again, to get out of bed, and go into the bathroom to put on her makeup. Foundation, beige. Tawny blush, then scrub most of it off with tissue. Red lipstick, a surprise addition on a conservative dresser. My mother has worn red lipstick for as long as I can remember. In and out of fashion. Summer or winter. Daytime or evening.

She called to my father insistently now, her voice louder because it was a school day and it was almost time for us to get up anyway. "Make the coffee, Ben!" She no longer let him stay in bed.

It sounds weird, but she talked to him like he was a troublesome child. Believe me, I can understand her exasperation. I know what it's like to have a father who is sitting in his chair, taking up space, but isn't really there at all. What must it be like to be married to him? I figure he was becoming the fourth child my mother never wanted.

"Where do you keep the coffee filters?" my father called from the bottom of the stairs. It's not like he hasn't been making coffee in the same Mr. Coffee machine for years. I mean, he sounded like me when I asked my mother which subway to take in the city, and my brain shut down over the simplest thing—East Side, West Side, what? I would feel like a total dummy, and my anger would fuel my inability to understand. Was my father angry too? Billy the jock psychiatrist says that anger is the other side of depression, but I watched my father for some glint of fury in his eyes, hopeful, because anger is so much realer than depression. You can yell back. Now my father sounded shut down, kind of East Side, West Side, Huh?

"I'll show you," I called to him. I threw on my bathrobe and went downstairs on my mini-rescue mission, found the coffee filters and popped one into the machine. "How many scoops?" I asked cautiously, steeling myself against that glazed look, that huh?

"I'm not sure," my father said, digging the scoop into the dark mound of coffee.

"I'll go ask," I said dully, and I shuffled to the foot of the stairs. "How many scoops?" I shouted.

My mother called down, "I can't hear you," and I repeated myself. "Four scoops, for God's sake; number eight on the pot for the water."

"I don't even drink coffee! How should I know?" I shouted. I returned to the kitchen and removed the scoop from my father's hand, scooped four measures of coffee, filled the pot with water up to the 8. My father stood there, back hunched over like he was eighty. He said quietly, "It's hard on your mother. It's hard on everyone." Then he flipped the switch on the coffeemaker, his contribution. "I can't seem to shake this thing," he added.

Like he had the sniffles. Or maybe even a hacking cough, a sore throat. A cold that lasted three long months, dragging on day after day, affecting every member of the family, only we weren't coughing or sneezing or wiping our runny noses.

"It's okay, Dad," I said. "We're doing fine." How could you get angry?

Angie didn't think I was doing fine at all.

"You're a real bitch lately," she said. "Alex really shook you up, didn't he?"

"Alex didn't. Alex and Lynn with their mouths glued together did. I just can't believe it." We were walking home from school, and Angie peered through the window of Seeger's Luncheonette. I examined the poster of a hamburger oozing catsup.

"That reminds me of Rachel's little accident on the rock," I told her, watching Angie screw up her face.

"Don't make me sick! I wanted to order french fries!"

"I can't help it if Rachel was traumatized by getting her—"

"Enough! We're going in. Your nemesis is in there."

"You've been studying Shapiro's vocabulary lists. My mother would kiss your feet."

Angie, always the brave one, pushed open the door. "Nemesis. One who imposes retribution, just punishment, or vengeance. Lynn."

I pushed after her, to the jangling sound of a hanging wind chime. "You make it sound like I'm the one who's done something wrong," I whispered.

"So maybe I used the wrong word," Angie breathed in my ear.

"Hiiiii," sang a voice from the corner.

"Hi, Lynn. Hi, Nancy," we sang back, sitting two tables away.

"Since when are they friends?" I growled at Angie.

"You'd rather it was Alex?" hissed my friend. "Split some french fries with me."

"A large diet soda," I told the waitress. "You get the fries and I'll eat one or two."

"Or three," said Angie, giving the waitress her order.

"Don't do me any favors," I said, the bitch again.

Angie raised an eyebrow. "Touchy, aren't we?"

The waitress put two glasses of ice water on the table.

"You know I'm trying to diet."

"Well, it puts you in a rotten mood."

"So tell me what's going right?"

"I don't know." Angie concentrated on balancing packets of sugar against each other. She built three houses.

"My dad is a nutcase. My mother is like . . . is like . . ." I swept my hand across the table, destroying Angie's village.

Angie tucked the sugar packets back into their container, saving them from me. "You never talk about your father," she said quietly. "I'm afraid to ask."

I didn't make it any easier for her. I drank ice water.

"What makes him a nutcase?" Angie looked intently at me. "I mean, what does he do?"

"He's not foaming at the mouth, if that's what you mean."

I was fighting it hard, talking about my crazy father to my best friend, because it didn't feel right. I felt like I was divulging top-secret information, like I was a double agent, and the guilt was spilling out of my ears. But Angie didn't care. She pressed forward, the inquisitor.

"What does he do all day long?" she said.

"He doesn't do anything. That's the trouble. He follows a list my mother gives him so that he doesn't just sit there all day examining his toenails." My double-agent stomach turned over.

"Is he a manic-depressive?"

Suddenly Angie turned psychiatrist. I turned bitch again. "Shit, Angie, he's depressed; there's nothing manic about it. Think of a turtle—you can get a picture of my father."

The french fries arrived, and Angie dipped one carefully into catsup. "My cousin is a manic-depressive," she said, looking injured. She popped the fry into her mouth. "When she's manic, she bakes cakes at three o'clock in the morning."

"My father does not bake cakes at three o'clock in the morning. He vacuums every day, about three o'clock in the afternoon, and there's nothing manic about it."

Angie wiped her mouth delicately with a napkin. "Why is he depressed?"

Everybody asked the same question. I remember my mother shrieking into the phone to Grandma on the other end, "His mother died five years ago, for heaven's sake." Then: "I know he's an orphan. His father died when we got married! That isn't why he's depressed."

"Let's just drop it," I said. Lynn and Nancy hovered in the corner of my eye, and I didn't want them to hear me.

"Well, my cousin got into a tailspin when she lost her job. Now she takes something, and she's okay."

"Maybe french fries would pull him out of it," I said flatly. It was pin-the-tail-on-the-donkey, and my father was the donkey. A death? Failure? Sickness? Bankruptcy? People wanted the answer desperately, so that they could say, "Oh, he's like that because . . ." It made them feel better if they knew they wouldn't catch it. They stuck my father full of pins with tags on them. His mother never showed him love. His father traveled a lot. They were very poor. They got rich too quickly. I listened and listened to the adults talk, and I came away with nothing.

"It's a chemical imbalance," I said. Maybe that would shut her up.

"Nothing's happened to make him—"

"Shit, maybe I did it!" I yelled. "Maybe he's disappointed in me. In the family. I mean, I don't help my mother enough, I talk back, I—"

"Now *you* sound like the crazy one," said Angie.

I pushed back so fast that the water glasses trembled. I scared myself, I really did, because I was ready to smash Angie in the face. My heart was beating furiously as I struggled to put on my coat. Angie grabbed my hand and held on to it.

"I didn't mean it," she said softly. "Don't run out of here."

I turned my head slightly and saw them through a blur of tears: Jimmy and Alex, standing in the doorway. I didn't remember hearing the jingle of the stupid chimes. Jimmy walked toward us in his practiced slouching tough-guy walk, and Angie pulled her hand away.

He raised an eyebrow. I sat back down.

"A little lezzie activity here, girls?" Jimmy said. Laughter surrounded him, bounced off the walls, off the ceiling, as the two boys joined Lynn and Nancy. I couldn't even look at Alex. I fastened my hand around a glass of ice water and drank some. Then I signaled for the waitress.

"Another order of french fries," I told her.

Angie didn't say a word.

We stayed long enough so that it didn't look like we were running away. I staggered outside into the daylight, light-headed and off balance, like a drunk leaving a bar. Angie treated me like one—solicitous, kindly, steering me down the street to a bench by the memorial for dead soldiers. Flowers were newly planted in the dark earth surrounding the black granite slab, and I scanned the alphabetical listing. Carney, Carr, Carter, Clavia. I landed on a Cohen, searching for the first name Ben. "Shit," I heard myself say.

"What?" said Angie, my nurse, braced for anything.

"I'm killing off my father," I told her.

She didn't question me. She began to laugh.

"What's so funny?" I asked her.

She shook her head and doubled over, her chin pressed to her chest as she continued laughing.

"Tell me!" I insisted.

"I was about to say that you're crazy again," she gasped, "but I stopped myself just in time." She slowed to a giggle and looked at my face to see if I would join her or kill her. I joined her, and it was a relief. It felt so good to laugh.

A boy walked past us and did such a double take that I was sure he'd noticed Angie.

He looked right at me. "Aren't you Professor Cohen's daughter?"

If he was handing me a line, he could have picked a better one than that. Angie collapsed into another fit of laughter, and I turned beet red.

"Yes." I looked at his face, a nice face, with stubble all over it.

"English lit. I met you in English lit. Freshman class."

"I'm a junior in high school," I said, blushing harder. Angie was moronic now, laughing like a madman. Madwoman.

"I saw you in your mother's class." He extended a hand.

Very hairy wrists. Cuteness descended from the apes. "Richie," he said. "Richie Pollan."

"Zoe," I said, shaking his hand and feeling like a jerk. "I'm surprised you remember me."

"You're hard to forget," he said, laughing. "Hey, can I call you sometime?"

"It's in the book," sang Angie.

He smiled and cast a brown-eyed look at me. "So would it be okay?"

"If you want," I told him. Why is it that I can write poetry about the wonders of nature—smell the flowers, see the sunset, feel the heat of the sun on my face—but I can't talk to a boy. No, a man. Hairy wrists, five o'clock shadow, black chest hair curling out of his shirt. Richie Pollan was a man.

Angie turned to me when he left. "Life's a bitch, isn't it?" she said.

He didn't call that week, and I filed his face away in my head as a failure. A failure on my part to be interesting enough to make him remember me. The thought occurred to me that he had remembered me once already. Then why had he so quickly forgotten me? It confirmed my uneasy dealings with the opposite sex. Reverse the situation, and I would have called him right away. Or at least the next day. I mean, he'd told me I was hard to forget. Angie and I debated that point. She said it must have been sexual attraction. I said maybe he needed a good grade from my mother. "What a suspicious mind you have," Angie told me. Secretly I hoped I was wrong. I asked my mother that evening.

"Richie Pollan. Richie Pollan. The name is familiar."

"He's hairy and cute. About Daddy's height, with biceps. Curly hair on his chest."

"Curly hair on his chest?" My mother mocked me. "Biceps? Now I recall him vividly."

"No, really, Mom." I pressed her again. "In your freshman English lit class."

"I do remember now," she said. "He dropped out."

"Dropped out? Did he give you any reason?"

"He told me I assigned too much reading. He switched to Heinmann's class because he said that Heinmann had a lighter load. I remember thinking that Heinmann could have him."

"Maybe he had a lot of work in his other classes."

"English was his major. If he doesn't want to do the work, why take it as a major?"

"Well, he asked me if he could call me."

"I guess he can. But wouldn't you think an English major would want to read?"

My mother was real snotty-looking, with an eyebrow hanging in the air. I said icily, "Not everybody can measure up to your standards."

She hesitated, and for a moment I thought she was going to tell me to watch my tone of voice. Then her face softened, and she said, "Well, maybe I just think he has lousy taste in teachers."

"So I can go out with him?"

"You can go," she said. "He seemed nice enough."

"Thanks," I said grudgingly, and I walked away.

"Zoe?" my mother called after me.

"What?" I shot back, like I couldn't care less if she answered me at all.

"He has excellent taste," she said, smiling.

"What do you mean?"

My mother approached me with her arms wide open. I knew she wanted to hug me, but it felt like the hugging part of me had shut down and you had to order the part from somewhere across the world, Japan or China. "He has good taste if he wants to go out with *you*," she said, letting her arms fall to her sides.

"Right," I told her.

"Is everything okay?" she said anxiously.

"I guess." I avoided her eyes and stared at one of Cara's flower paintings on the opposite wall. "How can you stand it?" I said.

She knew what I was talking about. "Your father?" she said.

I didn't answer, but my eyes wandered away from the framed vase of pink roses to my mother's pink-rimmed eyes.

"It's not easy," she said.

"He's not getting any better," I said. "You know he's not."

"I know." My mother put out her hand, her clean-scrubbed, round-nailed hand, and touched my chin, lifted it a half inch.

"How come you never wear nail polish?" I said to her, because I knew without looking that her nails were color-free. No scarlet nail polish for her, and why not? Why couldn't she break free, why couldn't she paint her fingernails and toenails and anything else she wanted to? Why didn't she want to? If I asked her, she would say, "What do you want from me? Do you want me to lie around and eat bonbons all day?"

Now my mother gave me a blank look, open-mouthed, and I sent her a zinger. "We're not a family anymore," I said.

"We are," she said softly. "He'll get better."

"What if he doesn't?" As I watched her face fall, it occurred to me that she looked as depressed as my father.

t e n

I walked the long way home from school a few days later. The lawns were sprouting poetry, they really were, even though I would never tell Margot, because she would think I was a nerd. Brainwashed by my parents never to pick flowers, I was glad to find a stranded blossom on the ground. I cradled it in my hand, sniffed it. Very little scent. I tucked it in my buttonhole, whatever it was. A magnolia blossom, an apple blossom? My father always knew. I could pick out the yellow flowers, the forsythias and the daffodils. I was good with yellow. And tulips. I guess everyone knows tulips, from way back in kindergarten, when you cut them out of colored construction paper.

Anyway, the lawns were sprouting poetry, the trees were in bud, and all was right with the world, because Richie Pollan had called. Shallow me. I mean, wouldn't it be better if an apple blossom could cheer me up?

My father had picked up the telephone, at my mother's command. "My hands are dirty, Ben. Please get the phone." She didn't ask him, she told him. From the dining room, I could see him holding the receiver like it was a foreign instrument. "It's for you, Zoe," he said quietly.

My mother poked her head around the corner, hands in the air like a surgeon. "I'm baking cookies, and I'm full of dough," she said. "It's for you." My mother never shouted from the other room anymore. It was a habit that bothered her too much, and she had finally held a conference about it. "Dad says it's a boy," she added in a whisper.

I half dragged myself into the kitchen. I wanted it to be Richie, but what would I say to him? When I took the phone from my father, he winked at me, kind of a B.C. wink, from back in the old days—before crisis. I didn't return the smile, but it registered.

"Hello?" I said, trying to keep the quivery feeling from my voice.

"It's the college boy who tried to pick you up in the street the other day."

"Oh, the one with the line about knowing my mother?" I glanced at my father and stretched the extension cord around the corner into the dining room.

"I do know her," he protested. "I know her so well that I quit her class!"

"She told me." I froze a little, because now he would know that I had talked about him.

"What can I tell you? Your mother is a slave driver."

"Tell me about it," I said, waiting for him to get to the point.

"Listen, the reason I called was, do you want to go to a jam session in the city next week?"

"Who's playing?" I said, hoping I would know the group and hoping I would sound musical. Maybe I should have said, Who's jamming? or, Where's the gig?

"Some friends of my brother, in a club in the East Village."

I stumbled a little. "Is there . . . I mean, do they play early?" I sounded like a moron.

"There's an eight-o'clock gig, the early set. I could get you home by . . . What time are youngsters like you supposed to get home?"

"What night are we talking about?"

"Friday. Not this Friday, but next."

I covered the mouthpiece with my hand and returned to the kitchen. "Mom, Richie wants to know if I can go to a concert with him in two weeks. It starts at eight o'clock. He could get me home by twelve at the latest." I held my breath and waited.

My mother looked at my father. "No later than eleven-thirty," she said firmly. "What do you think, Ben?" She consulted my father like an afterthought.

"Fine," said my father.

I wondered vaguely if he would have let me go B.C. "I can go," I breathed into the phone.

"Great. I'll call you a few days before."

And that was that. I was on my way home from school, the magnolias or was it the dogwoods were in bloom, I had a date with a college student, and all was right with the world.

My mother was outside the house, her winter coat unbuttoned. She was talking to her friend Rita.

"Oh, here she is," I heard her say, and I tried to imagine what errand she would send me on for poor Rita. Rita was still a wreck. In some perverse way, I think she made my mother feel better. My mother had a husband who wasn't there, but Rita had a husband who ran away. And my liberated mother could make it on her own, without a man. You could tell. She just happened to prefer the company of my father—who used to be funny until he turned half dead.

Anyway, I figured they'd send me running to Waldbaum's for Little Schoolboy cookies, Rita's favorite indulgence, or something like that. No such luck.

"Zoe, sweetheart," said Rita. "I have something to ask you. You don't have to say yes."

Did you ever notice how when somebody says, "You don't have to say yes," you always end up saying yes? I took one look at her pale, pleading face, and the word was on my lips already.

"Bert"—she swallowed some air when she said his name— "and I"—she gulped again at the linking of their names— "we'd already booked our bungalow for the weekend, you know, in Pennsylvania, past the Delaware Water Gap, where we—"

My mother stepped in. "I thought she should go. I mean, why should she stay home on such a beautiful weekend? She should go out and enjoy herself. They have hikes and bird-watching, and all the food is organized, lots of vegetarian, and I thought . . ." My mother lost her courage, and I didn't give her any help.

Rita rushed on. "Your mother figures that Bert is off having fun with this bimbo, so why shouldn't I use the reservation. I mean, it's paid for, and he's, after all, fooling around with this slut half his age."

My mother gave her a look. Protecting innocent me, I guess. Does she really think they don't have Rita's life plotted out on TV, a hundred times over on *The Young and the Restless* or *Santa Barbara*, where the husband leaves the gracefully aging fortyish wife for a younger, more supple bimbette? I hate to say it, but Rita's life was a cliché, and the revenge she was plotting was even more predictable.

"Would you go with me?"

I wasn't counting on that. I mean, I never included myself in the plot. Teenager Accompanies Jilted Wife on Rest Cure and Dies of Boredom.

"I've got a lot of homework this weekend, Mom." I tried to look imploringly at her, but she cast her eyes on poor Rita.

Rita spoke excitedly. "Oh, you can bring it with you—can't she, Lil? And there's a swimming pool—indoors, of course—and the food is good, lots of vegetarian . . . oh, we said that already, didn't we?"

Nancy Reagan's tired campaign slogan popped into my head, even though she's out of office, but I guess I could say no to drugs and sex a lot easier than I could say no to Rita Whiteman.

So I said yes.

I didn't bother to pack a bathing suit. Why torture myself? In fact, I took very little. Clean underwear, a toothbrush, makeup, the jeans I was wearing, a sweater, a nightgown. Who was I out to impress? The friend of Rita's who swept two strands of lanky hair across his balding egghead and pasted them on the other side? Or the one who thought he was a playboy, with the gold chains around his neck and the lame lingo that went back twenty-five years. "Lookin' groovy," he had told me when I met him at one of my parents' dinner parties.

I took along *King Lear* for when I got guilty, and a novel for when I got bored.

Rita behind the wheel made my mother look like a thirty-year-veteran driving instructor. She wove in and out of lanes, she honked her horn at slow drivers, she sang to the radio, and she chattered incessantly. She reminded me of Angie's cousin, the one who baked cakes in the middle of the night.

Hyper. She was going seventy miles an hour, and I was sitting right next to her.

"Slow down, Rita. You're making me nervous," I told her.

Rita looked surprised. She took a hand off the wheel and patted my knee reassuringly. "You're perfectly safe," she said. Her eyes widened, and she cried, "Oh, I love this song! 'Baby, just remember I give you my life. Forever one, when I make you my wife!' " She slapped the wheel and snorted. "That's a laugh, isn't it?"

I was amazed that she knew the words. My mother sings along with Mozart. But this wasn't her fun-loving friend, whom I'd known since I was a baby. This was some kind of human yo-yo, up one minute and down the next. I wondered why my mother hadn't noticed.

"Were things going wrong for a long time?" Maybe a grown-up conversation would snap her out of her giddiness, sober her up.

"I married him for better or for worse. Nursed the asshole through his heart attack. He was afraid to have sex for a whole year. I got him through it. I coaxed him back into those silk sheets that I spent a fortune on at Bloomies—I thought he'd have another heart attack when he got the bill, but I did it. No sex therapists like the ones you see on Oprah Winfrey, no psychiatrists, nothing. Just Rita. I got him primed and ready." Her face was contorted.

"Maybe he'll come back," I said lamely.

"Ask me if I'd have him!" Rita swung the car left into the fast lane, then cut off a refrigerated truck as she veered back into the middle. The blast of a horn followed us, and I resisted the urge to yell out the window, "I'm not with her!" I scrunched down in my seat.

"He could beg me on his knees, the bastard. He could cry buckets of tears, prostrate himself. I'd kick him out on his butt." Rita rolled down her window and stuck out her head. "Son of a bitch!" she screamed.

I was beginning to realize, with a queasiness in the pit of my stomach, that "Just say no" applied to more than sex and drugs. It meant Rita Whiteman too.

The bungalow wasn't at all what I'd imagined. No Laura Ashley prints and wicker furniture, with sunlight streaming through the window. No cat-shaped pillows and gauzy curtains blowing gently in the breeze. It was dark and spartan. Fake wood paneling, a brown-covered couch, decorated with vintage automobiles. Two cots in the next room. I mean cots, not beds.

"Sometimes the Girl Scouts rent these out, so they always use cots. Bert and I used to push two of them together, like a double bed. They started redecorating this one. . . ." Her voice trailed off as she waved a hand toward the couch. "Nobody else has a couch," she said. "But Bert and I like to read, and the bedroom is too dark. Well. That doesn't matter anymore."

"Is that why the bedroom is so big? The scouts?" The cots looked tiny in the huge expanse of room, lit by one small lamp on a crooked table.

"Sure. They can accommodate a dozen scouts in one of these rooms. Wait until you see the bathroom!" Rita ushered me into the brightest room in the bungalow. Bright yellow tiles with faded flower designs, a border of blue-and-white dutch tiles lining the top. And a large sunken tub, with steps.

"For Girl Scouts?" I said, amazed.

"Believe it or not, years ago this used to be a honeymoon colony. Everyone here was on their honeymoon. It used to be quite luxurious. Only the bathroom stood the test of time."

"Did you and Bert come here on your honeymoon?"

"Oh, heavens, no. We did the traditional route, Niagara Falls. Did you ever see that picture, with Marilyn Monroe and Joseph Cotten? He finds out his wife is having an affair. Every time Bert and I visited the falls, I saw Joseph Cotten prowling around and ready to pounce. It gave me the creeps." She laughed. "I should have told him—Bert—that my honeymoon gave me the creeps."

"What happens to Joseph Cotten?"

"Let me think. Oh. He takes some girl hostage and then just as they're going over the falls in a boat, he saves her."

"And he ends up in jail?"

"He ends up over the falls. Kaput."

I waited for Rita to tell me that Bert deserved the same fate, but she walked past me, into the living room. "The porch is actually quite comfortable, honey, if you want to read a little before we hit the dining room." She ran into the tiny kitchen and wet a paper towel. "Everything is usually a little dusty this early in the season." She swung open the porch door and wiped the only piece of wicker furniture in the house. "Sit, Zoe."

I pulled a book out of my satchel and settled in the two-seater. It was cushioned with soft pillows and swung a little, like the ones in an old Jimmy Stewart movie. Kind of romantic if you had the right person next to you.

Maybe Rita was thinking the same thing. "Comfy?" she said, looking at me with tears in her eyes.

"Fine," I said. I didn't ask her why she was crying.

The dining room looked a little like my high school cafeteria, except it was decorated with posters: Smokey the Bear putting out forest fires, and how to identify different trees and poisonous plants. I saw a few kids my age, already sitting down and eating with their families. There were lots of babies, crying, throwing french fries on the floor, toddling up to the dessert cart and sticking their fingers in the vanilla pudding. I could hear my mother's comment, something like "Children need discipline," and my dad would have joked, "Our children were perfect, weren't they, Lil?" He'd make her laugh, kind of depuritanize her. She's prune-faced now, maybe because he doesn't make her laugh anymore.

Rita and I joined a group of couples that she recognized. There was a chorus of "Rita! Where's Bert?" Rita just cocked her head and flipped out her hands, singing, "All gone!" like she was talking to a baby. They went back to eating their tuna sandwiches while we draped our coats over chairs, then joined the end of the food line. I was glad to get away from them.

When I reached the counter, I noticed the guy standing behind it. Dark hair and eyebrows, long eyelashes and beautiful dark-brown eyes. I could see his muscles ripple when he flipped a hamburger onto a bun. He must have flexed them on purpose, because let's face it, how much does a hamburger weigh?

He eyed me as I was deciding what to have, and I could feel my face turn pink.

"A hamburger, please," I said quickly, and when I looked up at him, he shook his head faintly.

"No?" I wondered vaguely what had happened to the vegetarian food.

"Pick again," he muttered under his breath.

"A hot dog, please."

He shook his head vigorously. "Ptomaine," he breathed.

"Tuna fish?"

The boy picked up an ice cream scoop and plopped a mound of tuna on a slab of whole-wheat bread.

"No rye?" I said.

"Stale," he said emphatically. "See you later."

I stepped lightly away, encouraged by the direction the weekend was taking. Back at our table, Rita bit into her hamburger ravenously. I noticed smugly that he had permitted Rita to poison herself. Not me. Me he had saved.

"I thought you were a vegetarian, Rita."

"Not since Bert," she said between bites. "I'm a carnivore now."

I didn't ask her if she planned on eating men alive from now on. "What are we going to do after lunch?" I asked instead.

"There's a nature walk, if you feel like walking off some calories. Then dinner—I think it's eggplant parmesan; it was posted on the wall over there. Pancakes for breakfast." Rita wolfed down some french fries, licking the catsup off her fingers.

I know what it's like to focus on food. I understand. When life sucks, food is a comfort. It doesn't judge you. It doesn't disappoint you. It just goes down your gullet and makes you feel full and warm. Sometimes I wonder if sex makes you feel that way, kind of fills you up, but without any calories. The movies seem to go either way. Sometimes when the couples make love, they eat ravenously afterward in bed, without worrying about crumbs in the sheets or cockroaches. And sometimes they moon around and don't eat a thing. I'd eat like a pig out of happiness.

A man leaned toward us from the other side of the table. "Say, Rita, I bumped into Bert in the city. He looked terrible! Burning the candle at both ends, I told him."

Rita just eyeballed him, and he added, "Wait till I tell him how good you're looking."

Sure. Vanilla pudding dripped from her mouth, and she washed it down with hot coffee. Rita was a picture of health.

She said, "Whatever you've heard about that bastard, I don't want to know." Then she pushed back her chair and steadied herself with a hand on my shoulder. Her wedding ring gleamed.

"I'm going for tea bags," she said. "Do you want any for your room, Ronnie?"

Ronnie shook his head, which threatened the strand of hair that was glued across his bald head. I watched him exchange glances with his wife, and I heard her mutter, "She looks awful."

Ronnie smiled grimly and looked at me, the shop dummy with no hearing. "It's Zoe, right?" he said. "I wish I could have convinced my son Toby to come. You're just his type."

But was he mine? I breathed a prayer of thanks.

Rita returned with a napkin full of cookies. "We might want them later. In the room, with our tea," she said triumphantly, tucking the white package into her purse.

"I was just telling Zoe that I was sorry Toby couldn't come. They'd make quite a pair."

"Oh, I don't think so. Doesn't Zoe need someone taller?"

I snorted my milk, but Rita kept talking. She was on a roll. "I know for a fact that she has a date with a college boy when we get back, and she's already won the counter boy's heart. Our Zoe doesn't need any matchmaking."

"You mean John?" said Ronnie's wife, Beth, red-polished fingers wrapped around her coffee cup. What were those fingers doing at this Girl Scout camp? They belonged at a ritzy hotel or something. "This is John's second year here, isn't it, Ronnie?"

Ronnie laughed. "Marcy was gaga over him last year."

Beth sipped her coffee and made a face. "The coffee is worse this year than last. It tastes like soap. Like someone cleaned out the urn and left the Ajax." She rested her eyes on me. "Marcy had a schoolgirl crush on him. Of course, she was only thirteen. You're a little older, aren't you?"

"I'm fifteen," I said hastily.

"Fifteen." She weighed the number in her mind. I held my breath. "Well. I know you're with Rita, but you're our responsibility too. We've met your parents a few times. I'd feel terrible if—"

Ronnie cut her off. "He's a responsible boy, Beth. He's saving his money for college, if I remember correctly."

"We're not talking about money here. There's a little matter of hormones."

"I'm sure he's a nice boy," said Rita, patting my shoulder.

"He's a hunk, and he knows it," said Beth. "He had Marcy wrapped around his little finger."

"I can take care of myself," I said.

"Of course you can," said Beth, raising the plucked arc of an eyebrow.

Rita changed the subject. "Are you people going to the square dance tonight?"

"We wouldn't miss it," said Beth. "Ronnie likes to allemande left with all the ladies."

"Good," said Rita. "I'm available."

"Of course you are," said Beth sweetly. "And aren't you lucky that you've brought a partner?"

It occurred to me that this group of adults didn't sound much different from my friends. More what you see isn't what you get, maybe. Rita the outcast, Beth the ringleader. I wasn't sure about Ronnie. The weakling? It seemed as if most men were beginning to look like that. The women took charge, like my mother, and the men followed. Bert Whiteman was no exception. Another weakling, hooked by the dental pick of a pretty hygienist.

"We're going to spend the afternoon by the pool," said

Beth. "Zoe, you're welcome to join us if you don't feel like hiking."

"Do, Zoe," said her husband.

I tucked an arm through the arm of Rita, my mother's oldest friend, and said, "I think I'd like the fresh air."

Rita smiled, and we went to join the other hikers.

eleven

*H*e was there at dinner. I saw him the minute we joined the end of the cafeteria line, a muscled beacon waving a serving spoon.

Rita noticed too. "Your boyfriend," she whispered, and I dug an elbow into her like she was Angie.

"I'm sorry," she said. "I'll keep my mouth shut. I just want you to enjoy yourself. I dragged you all the way out here, and I want you to have a good time."

"I'm having a fine time," I said. "The hike was great. I finally know the difference between a maple and an oak tree. My father will be thrilled."

"I haven't even asked you how he's doing."

"I heard him tell someone that he's hit a plateau."

"Well, that's good, isn't it?" Rita sounded a little uncertain. "A plateau sounds good."

"I guess." We moved along a few feet, and my heart started doing the dance it does when I have a crush on someone. "The eggplant smells good," I said to Rita, wanting to look animated. Maybe if we kept up a conversation, I could avoid looking at him.

I was facing him now, tongue-tied.

He made up my mind for me and filled a dish without asking. "Did you go on the hike?" he said.

"Oh." Was he talking to me? "Yes, I did."

"This will set you up," he said. He winked as he handed me the plate.

And that was that. He had said nothing about seeing me later. I'd missed my chance. The eggplant was tasteless, and Rita's eating habits were getting on my nerves. Worse, the seat I had taken meant that I couldn't see John at all.

I stood up and said, "I'm just going to return my tray," in the hope that I would catch a glimpse of him. I dragged my feet, scanning every corner of the cafeteria as casually as possible. He was nowhere to be found. And what would I do if I found him? Probably turn and run the other way.

I pushed the tray through the opening marked "Dirty Dishes." Black hands took it from me, sorted silverware from dishes, and threw them into the proper receptacle. They were not John's hands.

I returned to my seat and nibbled on a brownie Rita handed me. "They're great with milk," she said, sliding a glass toward me. I drank the milk.

Ronnie pushed back from the table and stood up. "See you all at the square dance," he said. He turned to his wife. "Come on, Bethie, let's get our duds on."

"Ready, partner?" said Rita, giving me a little tap.

"I really don't feel like dancing," I told her. "My feet still hurt from the hike."

Rita checked her watch. "We have an hour to rest up," she said hopefully. "Maybe by then . . ."

"I don't think so." I turned to go, and there was John, shirtsleeves rolled up to sleek muscles as he loaded a tray with dirty dishes.

He spoke to me as if we were in the middle of a conversation. "So I'll see you over at the hall tonight?"

"I think so," I said. Like I wasn't sure I would be there, like wild horses couldn't keep me away if I knew he was going.

"Save me a dance, then," he said.

"Sure," I called after him.

I heard a voice in my ear. "Smooth, isn't he?" said Beth. "But he doesn't know anything about square dancing."

"Why do you say that?" I asked her, ready to defend a boy I didn't even know.

"He would have asked you to save a tip for him. Fifteen minutes of dancing is a tip."

Ronnie crooned in my ear: "Maybe they won't dance," and he winked.

"She'll dance," said Rita brightly. "I'm her chaperone."

I had completely forgotten that I'd have to dance. Do-si-do your partner was the only call I knew. Get me the hell out of here was a stronger call. Dark-brown eyes and lean muscles were pulling me back.

"Tell me everything you know about square dancing," I said to Rita as we left the cafeteria.

Rita drove me crazy about what to wear.

"You can't wear jeans," she said. "There's nothing like a flowing skirt to make you look graceful."

"I'll look like a jerk."

"You'll look more out of place in jeans."

Rita laid a lavender skirt and a crinoline across the cot.

"I cannot wear that," I said ungratefully, eyeing the little dancing couples embroidered across the skirt. "It is definitely not cool."

"Do me a favor, your highness. Try it on."

I humored her. Shed my shirt and pulled on a white peasant blouse with puffed sleeves, straight out of *Heidi* or something. It drooped down around my shoulders, kind of like *Flashdance*. I never knew I had nice shoulders, but in the mirror, they looked creamy and round. Almost made up for no breasts, I didn't tell Rita.

"Put these on first." Rita handed me a pair of panty hose, the control-top kind, which made me feel like I couldn't breathe.

I slipped the full crinoline and the skirt over my head, ready for the chorus of dressing-room laughter you get when you put on an outfit and it looks so disgusting that you parade around in it to crack up your friends. Rita didn't laugh.

"Fantastic," she said, stepping back to admire her handiwork.

"I look like Carmen," I said, giving my hips a shake. "Without the cleavage." I looked so good I had to joke.

Rita dropped a pair of navy-blue Mary Janes in front of me. "Can you fit into a size eight?" she said. "You can't wear sneakers."

I'm an eight and a half, but I put them on.

A rainbow assortment of colored skirts brightened up the drab hall. I couldn't find John anywhere, for a dance or a tip or whatever you called it.

Rita was pink-cheeked with excitement, or maybe with rouge. Her breath smelled a little funny. What was in those four cups of tea she'd put away after the hike? She grabbed my hand, and we hooked up with enough people to make a square.

Beth was next to me. The only Beth I've ever known was the sweet one in *Little Women*, the one who nurses a sick baby and dies. Somebody screwed up when they named the Beth who married Ronnie.

"Where's your boyfriend?" she asked.

I shrugged my shoulders and was glad when the caller cleared his throat and pressed a button on his tape deck. The music began.

I picked up the calls faster than I expected. Dad always called Cara a quick study. Tonight, it was me. We danced three tips, and I did okay except when I craned my neck for John and missed a call.

"He'll show up," said Rita as we stood on line for coffee and cookies. "They're not all rotten," she added. Her smile didn't match her bloodshot eyes. I couldn't look at her.

I saw John over by the doorway. He was squinting his eyes and scanning the dance floor. Probably looking for blue jeans. I shot my hand into the air, praying that it was me he was looking for.

He waved back and weaved his way among colored skirts until he found me.

"Sorry," he said immediately. "They kept me late cleaning up, and then I had to get back and shower. You start smelling like . . . what did we have tonight?"

"Eggplant," I said.

"Well, I figured Eggplant by Oscar de la Renta just wouldn't do it."

I smiled and looked down at my Mary Janes. He had showered for me.

"Hey, I like your outfit. You look great."

"Thanks. Rita's idea."

"She's not your mother, is she?"

"No way!" I glanced around guiltily.

"She's talking over there. I mean, you don't look anything like her. She's short and you're . . ."

"Large?" It didn't take me long not to feel like Carmen anymore.

"Tall," he said. "Say, if you want to dance some more, I guess we should find a square."

"Do you want to?"

"Only if you do. Or if you want your feet stepped on." He grinned, twin dimples. How come it looks so great on a face and so lousy on a rear end? I felt like . . . what's that word they used in olden days? Swooning. I felt like swooning.

"Want to take some coffee and sit outside?"

I agreed, even though I hardly ever drink coffee. We grabbed our jackets and moved out to the porch, where we found a bench. I held on to my coffee cup for dear life, to hide my trembling hands and to keep from ruining Rita's peasant blouse. There were three inches between my skirt and his jeans. I counted them.

"There you are!" Rita poked her head around the corner. "I was wondering where you'd disappeared to."

"I'm here," I said, feeling foolish. I put an extra inch between us. The sight of the Mary Janes sticking out from under the bench made me feel ten years old, caught in the act of stealing chewing gum.

"Just let me know what you're doing," Rita said gently. "I'd better find a partner fast, for the next tip."

I nodded and waited until she left. I said out loud, "I feel bad for her."

John looked surprised. "How come?"

"Because her husband jilted her, and now I'm doing it."

"Hey, don't start beating up on yourself. You didn't make her husband leave her."

"But I'm keeping her company this weekend."

"Every minute of the day?"

"I guess not."

"So what are you worried about?" He moved his leg, and

we were an inch closer. "She's no spring chicken. Why do you think he left?"

"Because men are stupid," I blurted out.

"Present company excluded, I hope," said John, digging an elbow into my ribs. "She's no prize in the looks category, you know."

"Looks aren't everything," I said.

"They sure don't hurt."

"She just let herself fall apart after Bert left."

"If you ask me, they all let themselves go after marriage. Two of my sisters got married, had babies, and got fat. Turned me right off of marriage."

"Not everybody gets fat." I felt like I was about to start an argument with him. His muscles didn't matter anymore. We had moved at least half a foot apart.

He stood up. It was funny. Even though I wasn't sure I liked him anymore, my heart gave a lurch. He was leaving me.

He stretched. Not a care in the world, I thought, hating him. So go. Leave. "Want to take a walk?" he asked.

We started down the pebbled lane toward the cabins, when I remembered Rita. "I'd better tell her," I said, and I ran into the hall.

Rita was arm in arm with a bespectacled midget, at least three inches shorter than she was. The midget was smiling, and so was Rita.

I waited for her to allemande my way and tapped her arm.

"I'm going for a walk," I said.

Rita stepped in place as her partner twirled the adjacent lady. "Just be careful," she called.

"I'll meet you at the bungalow," I called back.

John was stamping his feet. "Come on, it's getting cold out here." He took my arm. We scattered pebbles as we walked.

"What college are you going to?" I asked him, steering the conversation away from fat wives and stupid men.

"Temple. I have friends in Philly, and it's a good school."

"Do you know what you're going to major in?"

"Probably poli-sci."

What the hell was poli-sci? I debated asking him but kept my mouth shut.

The gravel turned to smooth dirt, and we reached a cabin, smaller than the rest of the bungalows and a little larger than an outhouse.

"Home sweet home," he sang as he swung open the door and switched on the light.

Get me out of here, I thought, as I saw the single cot with a single pillow in the single room, with only a partition for the bathroom. I felt like I was visiting someone in prison.

"This is where they put the servants," he said, reaching into the closet for another pillow. He plumped the two of them against the wall, forming a makeshift couch.

"Sit," he said, waving his hand toward the bed with a flourish.

"Some wine?" He didn't wait for my answer but took the bottle off the shelf and uncorked it. Mutely, I accepted the glass he gave me, the same kind of cafeteria glass I'd drunk milk from.

"Sorry," he said. "No wineglasses."

"It's okay," I said, sagging back into the pillows in a peculiar position, my full crinoline flipping up around me. I clamped my knees together.

"Drink," he said. "Relax."

"I'm relaxed," I told him, watching the sediment float in my milk glass. I unclenched my jaw enough to take a sip. Sour grape juice.

"I'm not much of a drinker," I said.

"I can tell. Drink up. Chill out." He gulped down some wine and, walking over to the windowsill, switched on a radio.

"Background music," he said, smiling. "It's hard to create a little atmosphere in this dump."

I was ready for candlelight, I really was. He turned off the bare bulb and got down on his knees by the bed. What now, I thought, my knees still crunched together.

"Success," he said, pulling out a large flashlight and flicking on the switch. At least the light wasn't blue. He reached over and took my glass from me—maybe he'd seen the floating particles—but no, he was putting both our glasses on the floor, arranging his body next to me so that I could smell the grapy wine on his breath and see the stubble under his nose, and then his lips were on mine, and I forgot all about his muscles because I tasted coffee and wine and cookies, and oh God, I was back in biology class, with all the wetness, our tongues touching like slimy eels, and I thought, give me a toothbrush, somebody.

It didn't seem to bother John, but maybe boys are different, maybe they didn't mind the taste of old food in someone's mouth, because he kept on tasting and I tried to taste back, tried hard to forget about the eels, and my heart was pounding in my head as he pushed against me with an urgency that made my heart pound even more as I wondered when my sex drive would kick in like a motor, oh my God, wasn't I supposed to feel something, and now his hand was roving, now it was slipping so easily down my peasant blouse.

"Stop," I said, "stop," like Minnie Mouse, in a squeak so high that maybe only Martians could hear it—I mean, how loud was I supposed to say it? Do I say, Stop! I don't know you and I'm new at this and I'm not even sure if I like you and aren't we supposed to like each other, and where are my chaperones, get that hand out of my blouse, *I don't know you.* "Stop!" I said out loud, and his hand jumped out of my blouse and back onto my shoulder, and that was better, and he started tasting me again, and I tried to taste back but I wanted to go home because it was only a little better and maybe Cara was wrong, maybe I would never get used to it like avocado.

Then his hand, a foraging squirrel now, jumped down the elastic of my skirt, so easy to get into, no snaps, no buttons, damn Rita, damn this awful square-dancing skirt with the whirling couples on it, get me out of here, get me out of here. "What the hell is this?" a voice was saying, and it wasn't mine so it must have been his, and the hand was struggling now, trying to force its way down a pair of steel-trapped control-top panty hose, and it stopped.

"What the hell is this?" he repeated. "A girdle?"

I took advantage of the lull and gathered my skirt together, pushed off with my hand against the wall. "I really have to get going," I said.

"Now?" He sounded exasperated, amazed. "Now?" he repeated.

"Rita will be worried," I said, shaking my skirt into shape, brushing against a milk glass of wine, hearing it topple, looking for the door by the glow of the moonlight through the window and the gleam of the flashlight from the floor, and— exiting, making wine prints on the smooth dirt walk and on the pebbly gravel road—whispering, "Thank you, Rita, thank you," for making me wear the control-top reinforced elasticized steel-trapped panty hose.

I ran back to the cabin, reprieved, happy to see its ugly exterior. I let myself in quietly, in case Rita was sleeping. The living room, dark in the daytime, was pitch black. A rustling noise on the couch made my heart jump. A raccoon? A bear, for God's sake? There was a thump, and the sound of something rolling across the floor. As my eyes adjusted to the darkness, I could see a bottle dimly reflected in a sliver of moonlight.

"Rita?" I said softly. "I'm back."

A low moan came from the direction of the couch. Was that Rita's body sprawled across it?

"Rita?" I felt on the wall for the light switch, fervently hoping there were no spiders waiting. I would have made a lousy Girl Scout. I found the switch and flipped it on.

"Off, off," said the crumpled figure on the couch, and I obeyed her, switching us back into darkness.

"Are you okay?" I asked her.

"Fine, fine, I'm fine," she answered, pulling herself upright. "How you?"

Me fine. Me Jane, leave Tarzan in the lurch. "I'm okay," I said. I watched her rub her eyes, run a hand through her hair. I assessed her condition and decided not to confide in Rita Whiteman, my mother's best and oldest friend, tipsy on the couch.

"Was he nice? The kitchen boy."

She was trying to sound like a parent, which didn't hold much water with me because parents are overrated anyway. I addressed her as if she was a child. "The kitchen boy was fine. Why don't you go to bed, Rita?"

"Did you have a grand time? Bert and I always had a graaaand"—she stretched the word into three syllables at least—"time. He always laughed when I said a grand time. Said I sounded like a first lady or the queen or something." She lifted her hand into the air, orchestrated the words. "A graaaand time. We had a grand time." She sliced the air with her hand again, and her head lurched forward, following the movement.

I walked over and picked up the bottle.

"Apricot brandy," said Rita. "We liked a nightcap together. A nightcap. A cap on the night. Funny." She patted the sofa. "Sit, honey. Keep me company."

I sat and caught a whiff of her breath, apricot sweetness, not grapy and sour like John's.

"Ahh, there's nothing like young love."

I kept quiet. They let drunks ramble on in the movies, or they made them sip coffee. I let her talk.

"Bert said I was a great kisser. Did he kiss you? The kitchen boy, I mean, not Bert." She turned and looked at me seriously. I mean, her head didn't wobble. "You're still a little young for him. Bert. I'll give you five years or so." She moved her face a few inches from mine. "Did he kiss you?"

"Only once, at the door," I lied glibly.

"Bert was a lover, right from the start. Told me good things come in small packages, on our first date. I always hated being small."

"That was nice of him."

"Covering up. He was not too"—she paused, put on a regal expression—"not too well endowed in a certain department, if you know what I mean." She drew back, put another few inches between us. "But you're too young and innocent to know."

I didn't want to know. All your life, they tell you, Wait until you grow up, you can do it all when you're an adult, when you reach maturity. You can do what? You can become a space cadet of a father, a wreck of a wife, an iron lady of a mother?

I remembered *Peter Pan*—they showed it on TV a few

years ago—and Mary Martin is over forty and pretending she's a boy when she looks like a lady even though her thighs don't shake too much and she must have breasts as small as mine, and that stupid little light starts looking like a fairy even though you know it's a stupid little light, and Peter starts singing in his soprano voice, "I won't grow up, I won't grow up, I don't want to be a man, I don't want to be grown up," or something like that, and it didn't matter if he was a boy or a girl or a grown-up lady, because at that moment, with Rita's wobbly face a few inches from mine, I completely agreed with him.

twelve

My mother grilled me like a detective when I got home. "So what did you do?"

"We hiked, we ate. You know." I drank a cup of tea in my mother's large robin's-egg-blue kitchen, thankful to be home.

"And how was Rita?" She looked at me peculiarly.

"Why?" I took a bite of an oatmeal cookie, let my mother squirm a little. "Why do you ask?"

"She looked terrible when she dropped you off."

"She drank like a fish." I really don't know how much she drank, but it sounded good.

"I should never have let you go."

"No, you shouldn't have, should you?" I was not going to make her feel better. Not yet.

"Rita mentioned you met a boy."

"John. A lech." I watched her face for its anguish level. High.

"Oh my God. I'm so sorry. I don't know what I was thinking of, Zoe. Are you okay?"

"Just say no, Mother. Isn't that what they teach you?"

My mother sighed. "I was stupid, Zoe. I hope you can forgive me. Your father has been driving me—" She stopped abruptly.

"I know." She looked a little wild-eyed, pale-faced, only a left-over outline of red lipstick on her lips. She held her arms out to me. "*Can* you forgive me?"

I hugged her, sniffed my mother's Shalimar neck. Her breath smelled of toothpaste.

I never told Angie about the eels, but by the time I saw her at school, I had honed my weekend into a great story. It made Angie laugh until she was pink in the face. I could forget how scared I was, I could push to the back of my mind that it wasn't much fun, because I was experienced now. You couldn't count the time I was felt up in front of Macy's window, looking at Santa's sled dipping down on a rooftop while a hand was dipping up my skirt—until Angie noticed and yelled, "Cut that out!" so loudly that the man ran away. That didn't count.

"So what did I miss?" I asked Angie as we headed for the school cafeteria.

"Margot and I went to Grumpy John's for a while, and it was dead, so we went back to her house and watched a video." Angie loaded a tray with potato chips, a container of whole milk, chocolate pudding with whipped cream, and a grilled cheese sandwich, but that was deceptive. I knew she wouldn't eat half of it.

I filled a large container with lots of ice and diet soda, took a mound of cottage cheese. My tray was a still-life study in blandness.

"Revolting," said Angie.

"I totally agree. I ate like a pig over the weekend."

"You needed the energy!"

I liked the joking. Reading a diary is one thing. Watching all the moaning and groaning on television is another. And hearing Margot talk about it was just not the same as when it was happening to you, even if it did remind you of biology class.

"Did I tell you how I brushed my teeth twice when I got back to the cabin?" I milked my story again.

"You crack me up, Zoe."

Margot was waving at us, and we took our trays to her table. She made a face at my cottage cheese. "Oh, gross!" she said. "Don't make me barf!"

Angie defended me. "This girl is hot and heavy into dating. She's got to get her body into tip-top shape."

Margot raised an eyebrow. "With who?"

"A Uniondale guy. Zoe is into college boys now, aren't you, Zoe?"

"I hope Richie will be an improvement on John," I said.

"Richie? John? One at a time, Zoe." Margot jiggled the ice in her glass and raised it to her lips. "I saw Jimmy again," she said between crunches.

"I thought you were going to dump him. Because of his wandering eye."

Margot shrugged. "It wandered back to me," she said. "Lynn and Alex are definitely a couple now. Jimmy said he was only sampling the merchandise for Alex."

My cottage cheese tasted rancid. "Nice friend. What is she, a slab of meat?" I said.

Margot shrugged and picked at a few of Angie's potato chips. "We went to the movies. We went to the river. We had a good time."

"Was Lynn there with Alex?" I couldn't resist. I knew that Richie was in the near future, but Alex the Roman god still had me dancing on a string.

Margot raised her other eyebrow. "I thought you were busy with your college boys."

"I am. I just happen to think that Alex is kind of cute." Now that I was experienced, I felt I had a right to express my preferences. Angie looked surprised, but Margot took it fine.

"He's hot, all right. But he wasn't there. Just me and Jimmy and the river."

The river was the local parking spot. Cara and Billy used to go there to practice their avocado kisses, according to Cara's diary. It was kind of a rite of passage in town. I felt closer to reaching the river than ever before. I could see the weeping willow, with its branches dipping gracefully into the water. I could hear the car radio, turned way down, and the soft sounds coming from the back seat. I just couldn't see who was sitting next to me.

t h i r t e e n

I'm glad I have a big sister. Like I said, first-born children do all the rotten stuff first—go to the dentist, start kindergarten, knock on the door at Halloween, get a summer job, even French-kiss. Character-building stuff. Then the second-born toddles along and sails right through. So I should feel thankful to Cara, shouldn't I?

But lately, Cara is my friendly enemy. It's like she's there but she's not there. Not blank-faced, like my father; just rushing through.

It was six o'clock, and I had butterflies in my stomach as I waited for Richie to pick me up. I told Cara.

"Just have a good time," she said. "Be yourself."

What happens—at seventeen, everybody starts talking like a grownup?

"What if he starts something after the concert? Do I let him?" I sat on her bed and leaned my head against the wall.

"Do you want him to?" Cara brushed her hair, head hanging down between her legs, and gathered it into a ponytail.

"How do I know? John felt me up, and it was like he was

squeezing a cantaloupe or something. I mean, I didn't feel anything."

"Do you like this bow?" Cara tied a red silk ribbon around the ponytail and turned her back on me.

"It won't last half an hour. It will fall out." I was beginning to hate Cara and hate anything she put on. I took her stuffed snake and wound it around my leg like a boa constrictor.

Cara whipped the ribbon out of her hair and slipped an elasticized flower around the ponytail. "How's this?"

"Carmen Miranda Cohen." I threw the snake aside and banged my head slightly against her wall. Would she pick up on my sign of displeasure?

"What's eating you?" Cara fixed a pair of mascara-fringed eyes on me. "Don't get grease on my wall."

"My hair is squeaky clean," I said in a withering voice, and I crawled off her bed with as much dignity as I could muster.

Cara put out her hand like she was going to stroke a dog. "Look, I'm sorry," she said. "Billy and I are having problems."

"What kind of problems?" I asked, but I wasn't sure if I wanted to know. If the golden couple couldn't make it, then how could I, Dorothy Gale, meek and mild, from Kansas?

"Billy's pushing me a little."

"Pushing you?" I sounded dumb.

"He wants me to go all the way." She fiddled with her ponytail again, as if adorning that stupid hank of hair with the right decoration would solve all her problems.

"Try the barrette with the geometric designs," I said. What to tell Cara about entering the great and powerful land of Oz, the kingdom of sex, was beyond me. After all, I was only the middle child. How would I know?

Richie arrived promptly at 6:45. I opened the door and let him in. His dark stubble was gone, and I wondered if he had shaved for my mother or me. His ex-professor came into the hallway, and we followed her into the living room.

"It's nice to see you again," she told Richie. He extended a hairy wrist to her and she took it. "Ben?" She released his hand and walked to the kitchen. "Come and meet Richie," I heard her tell my father.

He drifted toward us in a semi-shuffle and tripped over the doorjamb, but he saved himself from falling with a hand on the wall. Then he straightened himself and held out the same hand to Richie.

"Ben Cohen," he said formally. "It's nice to meet you."

"They're going to a concert," said my mother. "I told Zoe that I want her home by eleven-thirty at the latest."

"Fine," said Richie. He consulted his watch. "We'd better get going."

My mother and father trailed us to the door in some kind of slow-moving ceremony, like I was leaving home forever and they had to say a blessing over me. As the screen door closed, I heard my mother say, "You're always tripping, Ben. You'd better talk to the doctor about your medication."

"What's the matter with your father?" was the first question Richie threw at me as we entered the car.

"Nothing," I said.

"Not too steady on his feet, is he?" Richie revved up the car the way some guys do. You know, you're not sure if they really need to make all that noise.

"Eye medication," I said. "He's having trouble with his eyes."

Richie nodded. "My father has a cataract. He's having laser surgery on it as soon as it gets a little bigger or something."

"I'll tell my dad," I said, and I was glad that Richie didn't catch the sarcasm. Do they do laser surgery of the brain? Zap—you're happy again. Zap—you can talk to your daughter again. Zap—you're a family again.

"Modern technology. I wanted to be a doctor, but my grades weren't too good in the sciences. You're into writing?" he said, veering onto the highway marked "Route 1-9, New York City."

"I'm into *living*," I said, holding on to the seat as he ignored the Yield sign and increased his speed. "The truck!" I said in a high voice, uncool. Where was the daring side of my personality, the part that was supposed to like thrills and danger, fast cars and downhill racing, not to mention making out.

"Take it easy," he said. "I see it."

John had told me to chill out. Richie wanted me to take it easy. I felt like a fearful little prune sitting next to a hot tamale. I worried my way through life, while the tamales sped into the fast lane.

We parked in front of a small café called Brownie Points. Through the plate-glass window I could see a case loaded with desserts. I made a mental note of it; maybe we'd want to get ice cream afterward. But did you eat ice cream after a gig? Probably not. I was being uncool again.

Richie consulted a scrap of paper, and we started walking. The street was lined with people in rags, sprawled on the sidewalk, leaning against walls, groaning, sleeping. Richie stopped in front of a blanket. Three wrinkled shirts were carefully displayed, arms stretched out like Christs on the cross. Six books lay side by side, and Richie picked one up and read the front flap. A bearded man, sitting cross-legged like a dirty guru, reached out his hand as Richie bent to replace the book. "I'll take it," he said. He curled blackened fingers around it. I watched as his hand touched Richie's. Cooties! rushed into my head, the game we played as children when we made believe someone had terrible germs. Now Richie took my hand, and I resisted the urge to pull away.

"So many homeless people!" I said as we walked away.

He shrugged. "There's a shelter somewhere around here. My brother petitioned against it."

"Why?" I was half-expecting a blackened hand to reach out and grab my ankle.

" 'Why?' " Richie looked at me as if I was a moron. "Would you like a bunch of bums living next door to you?"

"I guess not." Still, it seemed a little heartless to me. I was squeamish but not uncaring. Where were they supposed to live? Marooned on an island? I said, "They have to live somewhere."

"Oh yeah? How would you like to have the value of your apartment lowered by a bunch of lazy pissers?"

Full of compassion, I thought. He would have made some doctor.

The Dead End Café looked just like its name. Empty and airless. A handful of people sat around tables, smoking and holding glasses. Someone was setting up a huge amplifier on a makeshift stage, a cigarette barely touching the corner of his mouth. How did he keep it from falling out? Richie picked a table directly in front of the amplifier and gestured for me to sit down. I stopped myself from brushing off the chair, remembering a program I'd seen on obsessive-compulsive behavior, where you feel like you have to wash your hands four hundred times a day. The psychiatrist said it could start anytime. I didn't want it to start on my date with Richie. Quietly, imperceptibly, I did some deep-breathing exercises.

A man with tousled, Orphan Annie red hair stepped up on the stage and picked up a six-stringed guitar. He started strumming it. The sound was high, sharp, and piercing, and it spat straight out of the amplifier at us. I shot a look at Richie, but he ignored it. We weren't moving.

He leaned over toward me and said, "See that six-stringer? That's a Strat."

"A Stradivarius?" I said in amazement. "I thought that was a violin!" I realized my stupidity too late.

Richie rolled his eyes. "It stands for Stratocaster, dear."

Dear. Oh, wonderful, romantic, my great-aunt in the nursing home.

Another man was holding a four-stringed boxy-looking guitar. His spiky, bleached-white hair moved ever so slightly when he played, like stiff grass in the wind.

"That's the bass," said Richie. "Paul McCartney style. See? He's a lefty."

I was thrilled by that piece of information and stored it away for the future.

"What are you drinking?"

"A diet Coke," I said, holding my breath.

"A rum and Coke," said Richie to a woman all in black, including black lipstick. "And a beer. Whatever you have on tap." She nodded, and I watched Richie watch her. He turned toward me again, resting his chin on his hand, his elbow in a small puddle of unknown origin. I pointed to it, and he lifted his arm away as I mopped it up. So now I was a house-maid.

"Your mother said you want to be a writer," said Richie.

"I try," I answered, wondering if I would throw up the rum and Coke. It arrived, and I sipped it.

"Good?"

I nodded. Disgusting. You're a bastard for changing my order.

"Loosen up," he said.

I clenched my teeth and concentrated on watching the redhead and the young Andy Warhol, until finally the keyboardist arrived and nodded his head vigorously—one, two, three—and the music began. Pulsating, ear-boggling, mind-drowning noise. I searched for a melody and came away empty. I rotated my shoulders, bopped my head to the pounding sound, syncopated it with "I Hate Men, I Hate Men." Richie looked like he was enjoying himself. I continued my pulsing "I Hate Men." I thought of my father.

We left the café, if that's what you call it (a café sounds like Paris in springtime, and leaving the Dead End was like leaving a tomb). My uncoolness changed quickly to downright nervousness as Richie took my hand again and we traced our way past the bums and the garbage.

He stopped to kiss me once, tongueless, but a reminder that at a mere 9:30, the evening was just beginning.

"Where to?" said Richie, rubbing his thumb on the top of my hand.

"Home?" I said in a small voice, Dorothy again, and ready to recite my mantra: There's no place like home, There's no place like home, There's no place like home.

"Home it is," said Richie, and I was surprised. I never thought he'd be my good witch. I thought he'd roll his eyes again.

The highway was empty. Most of the traffic was heading for New York City, and we were leaving it, thank goodness. Maybe it was gratitude, but I felt a little closer to Richie. He may have ordered a spiked drink for me, against my wishes, but he was taking me home. I made a half-turn with my head and checked out his profile. A slightly pouty lower lip, a straight nose, hooded dark eyes. A little like mine, but wilder, like Jack Nicholson when he plays devils. Not a bad-looking face. A college boy. So how come my heart wasn't thumping for him?

He turned and caught my eye and tried to pull me toward him, until I was almost strangled by my seat belt.

I should have known. Richie is a townie, and he knows his way around. We reached the river in record time.

He flipped open my seat belt and scooped me over to him, already a different kisser than John, a rougher kisser. This time I knew enough not to expect a clean mouth; I braced myself for the taste and the rolling of the tongue. I was ready for the hands trying to run their fingers through my hair. Didn't college boys know that after three hours, if your hair hasn't been combed it's practically impossible? His hand got stuck halfway down, and he clasped his fingers around the back of my head, like I was a basketball or something. He stroked my eyebrows with his thumbs. That was different. John never did that. "Furry little things," he murmured, and I wondered if it was a compliment.

His hand wandered down to the zipper of my jeans, skipping step two, the feeling-up part, completely. It startled me. Wasn't he even interested in my breasts? The deftness of his movement made my heart beat furiously. Oh my God, the river of no return. Date rape. Keep calm. I put my hand on top of his. "Wait," I said. His hand obeyed as he continued kissing me. Less than a minute later, it started moving again, and I squeezed his hand hard. "Stop," I said.

"Why?" he said.

"I'm scared," I told him. Maybe he would take pity on me. Maybe I could go home now.

"Don't be scared," he said softly, and he reached his hand inside my pants and wiggled his way down until he could hook his index finger inside me, no control-top panty hose obstructing his way. He started stroking me, this time for more than a minute, and I waited tensely for the dam to break, for the tidal wave to rush in and sweep me away, for the earth to give way. Nothing. I was as quiet as a mouse.

His mind must have jumped, like a computer, to Reprogram, Discontinue Process, and he pulled his hand out of my pants and took my fist and unfurled my fingers and held it against his bulging jeans. "Unzip it," he whispered, but my hand was paralyzed, I know it was, because I willed it to respond and my index finger was stuck to my thumb with instant Krazy Glue, and in a trembling palsy I could not grip the zipper and pull it down.

"I'll do it," said Richie impatiently, and I heard the zipper catching on metal but my eyes were squeezed shut by now, and I was blind and crippled, but not deaf, because I heard him say, "Look at it," and I knew I couldn't get pregnant from looking, I knew I couldn't get AIDS, either, but I wouldn't look, instead I groped in the dark for the door handle. Then I heard him say, "Kiss it!" and I heard myself say, "No way," and my head was reeling as I heard him laugh, and I found the door handle and opened the window instead of the door, which made me think of air, I needed some air, and I heard myself say, "I need some fresh air."

Richie fiddled with his pants and put it away like some jack-in-the-box, except I was afraid of Jack and gratified, ecstatic, elated that he was back in his box. Richie the smart college boy who once wanted to be a doctor had the compassion of a stone, because he snorted and said, "Never mess with jailbait." Then he started the car, pulled out of his space with pebbles flying, and took me home.

I let myself out of the car and called to him, "Thanks!" like a moron. Give me a break! Thanks for giving me a heart attack? Thanks for nearly splitting my eardrums? Thanks for confirming that I'm not normal because there wasn't one thing that I did with you that made my heart sing, or whatever hearts do when they like sex.

As I reached the top of the stairs, I heard my mother call from her bedroom, "Is that you, Zoe?"

Her door was closed. "It's me," I answered, heading straight for the bathroom, because I felt like heaving. I took a swig of vanilla creme antacid and swallowed it down.

My mother persisted. "Did you have a good time?"

Don't call from the other room, I felt like telling her, but I didn't say it, because then she might come out and look in my eyes and ask me what was the matter, and how could I tell her with that dead-eyed stranger in bed next to her?

"I had a grand time," I said to the door. "I'm going to sleep."

"Good night," said my mother.

"Good night, honey," said a voice that was my father's.

fourteen

*A*ngie was a good listener. As we walked into town, she nodded at the right places and widened her eyes when I meant her to. She stopped abruptly in the middle of the sidewalk as I came in for the finish. "Don't tell me," she said, putting a hand out, her mouth round and open and waiting. She clutched at me, and I wanted to tell her what she wanted to hear, that I was Madonna and Barbie and Cher and Zoe, all rolled into one.

But I wasn't, so I turned mysterious and tantalized my audience of one by saying, "You don't want to know," except I couldn't look at Angie, and she was certainly looking at me. I waited, but her eyes were boring into my head, until finally I said to her in a small voice, "Have you ever seen one of those things, full blown?"

"Only in my cousin's *Playgirl*," said Angie, "and it was tiny."

I watched out of the corner of my eye as she picked a sprig off a privet hedge and pulled off one leaf at a time, crunching each in half as she let it fall to the ground. Angie waited patiently.

"I couldn't—" I stopped short. "I mean, I saw one a long time ago, and I remember that it was . . ."

"Humongous," said Angie helpfully.

"Humongous," I echoed. "But I couldn't look. I closed my eyes like I was watching a horror movie and I didn't want to see the scary part."

"You're entitled," said Angie. "Who does he think he is, anyway?"

"God's gift to the world, that's who." I was feeling a little better. I stole a look at my friend's face and said, "He told me to kiss it."

"I'm going to barf," said Angie, and it was the best thing she could have said, because she didn't like the idea any better than I did, and I wasn't crazy or frigid or undersexed, and Angie said, "I hope you said no!"

"I said, 'No way!' " I told her, laughing.

"He must have laid an egg," said Angie, screeching with laughter.

"I didn't stick around to find out," I said solemnly, and that made Angie laugh more.

"Hey," said Angie, composing herself. "If we walk down High Street, we can pass the scene of the crime."

"No way," I said.

"Come on," said Angie, pulling me past a row of houses that reminded me of a song my father used to sing, about little boxes made of ticky-tacky, way back when he used to sing.

"No, no," I protested. "Don't make me. It might still be there!" I pulled away in mock terror as Angie made a megaphone with her hands, calling in a deep voice, "Snake, snake, is there a snake in the park?" She ran ahead, jumping out at me from the bushes, screaming "Snake!" until my heart started pounding for real, and I shouted "Stop!" as if it was Richie instead of Angie.

Angie sat down on the grass and started to laugh, with her head in her hands, and I sat down next to her, stony-faced, because she didn't understand, until I looked at the ground next to her and shouted, "Oh my God, don't move!"

Angie followed my pointed finger to the spot on the ground and said, "Oh, gross me out, can I get pregnant from that thing?" as we gazed at the spent pink condom nestled in the green grass like a crocus.

"Let's get out of here," said Angie, and she pulled me to my feet and back onto the sidewalk, and suddenly we were kids again, singing, "Lions and tigers and bears, oh my!" I stepped in rhythm to another song that my father used to sing as I made up my own brand of hopscotch, only one foot allowed in each block. "Step on a crack and you'll break your father's back," I said to myself.

We reached town and headed for Choux-Choux's, the only decent clothes store around, unless you drove to the shopping mall. The ladies behind the counter looked a little like the name of the store, fake French, with dark painted lips and short sleek hairdos, but when they opened their mouths, it was New Jersey.

Angie and I shared a dressing room and tried on some marked-down T-shirts. "I can't even afford the markdown," I whispered to Angie.

"I'd let you borrow, but that shit-brown color looks awful on you."

We were full of mirth again, snorting and smirking our way through the sale rack, until Angie announced, "I need a bra!" A fake-French lady stood up and came over to us. "May I help you with the lingerie?" she said, her lips in a pout.

"Double A," said Angie, pouting back.

"I think Playtex has a brassiere for you," said the lady. "Their Right for Me series. The almost A."

"Almost A? I'll try it." She took the brassiere that the lady dangled in front of her. "No lace?" Angie made a face. "My boyfriend likes lace."

"The smaller sizes tend to . . ."

"Never mind. I'll try it on." We went back to the dressing room, and Angie pulled off her sweatshirt.

"An A-minus bra with no lace on it," said Angie, fastening the bra in front of her and sliding it around. She shrugged her arms into it and turned toward the mirror. The bra drooped around her breasts.

"No romance," she said glumly.

"Richie didn't even check out my bra," I said, trying to be helpful.

"John did, didn't he?"

"It was so dark, he didn't even see it."

"Really?" She brightened a little. "Maybe if I get it in black?"

"Get a pretty sports bra, the stretch kind. That way, when your bra straps show, it's a bright color."

"But I'm not the sporty type," said Angie.

"That's okay. You'll look sporty in it. Haven't you ever noticed that athletes have tiny boobs?"

"All muscle, you mean. Do boys like that?" Angie turned her back to me. "Unfasten me."

The hooks were stiff, and I wondered how boys did it. "Cara and Billy watched the women bodybuilders on TV the other day, and Billy said they were very sexy."

Angie slipped off the bra and handed it to me. "Could you give this to Mademoiselle Bowwow out there? I need to go to the drugstore for shampoo. Anything but Breck's. My mother has had me on Breck's since birth."

"No wonder your boobs are so small."

Angie laughed, and I went to return the bra. I guess that's what my friendship with Angie is all about. We don't lie to each other, but we try to make the best of the truth.

At Bell's Pharmacy, Angie went straight to the shampoo section and started rummaging.

" 'Hair so soft and free,' " she said. "Sounds like it will lift right off your scalp."

"Richie tried to run his fingers through my hair."

"Romantic," said Angie, fingering an iridescent bottle that looked like it would glow in the dark.

"They got stuck," I said. "In the tangles. Maybe I'll pick up some conditioner."

"For the future?"

"For tangles," I said, in my mother's the-subject-is-closed voice.

Angie made her selection, something hip and zippy that promised a fuller love life, and I picked up a fifty-nine-cent "complimentary-size" protein conditioner. We heard voices rising at the back of the store, and one of them sounded familiar.

"I didn't do anything," the voice protested shrilly. It was my sister Rachel.

"If you didn't do anything, what's the lipstick doing in your coat pocket?" said a man in a white coat.

"I don't know how it got there," said my sister dully.

I knew she was lying. I stiffened my big-sister shoulders and headed for the man in the white coat, with Angie on my tail.

"What's the matter?" I said to the white coat.

"Who are you?"

"She's my sister," said Rachel quickly, and up close I could see tears in her eyes.

"I'm her sister," I echoed, and I looked at the lipstick the man held out to me. The wrong shade, but I didn't say so.

"I found this in your sister's pocket. She left the store with it, and I've told her I'm going to call the police."

Rachel turned her deep-set eyes on me. They looked just like my father's, and maybe someday she would get depressed too, because she sure was making a mess of her life, but right now I had to save her.

"Please don't call the police," I said. "She knows she did wrong. I'll take her home and tell my parents." I don't know why I added the last part. I guess I thought he wouldn't think I'd punish her on my own. Angie stood next to me, my friend, my ally, her zippy shampoo in her hand, and said, "We'll take her home."

"I'm afraid I can't let you do that," said the man, and my heart dropped. "Give me your phone number, and I'll call your parents."

I gave it to him. "Listen," he said, and his voice was a little softer. "I'm a parent. I have kids of my own. But you can't just let your children run wild."

I heard my voice get huffy. "They don't let us run wild," I said, clutching the tiny bottle of conditioner in my fist.

"The parents work all day, and the children run loose. Look at her!" He pointed to my sister. "A young girl like her, stealing my merchandise! What the hell is this country coming to?" He picked up the phone. "What's that number again?"

We watched him dial. He jiggled the wire as he waited for someone to answer the phone. My heart was beating furiously. I felt like I had committed the crime. My mother was giving a seminar, I knew that. The man in the white coat was talking now.

"She's right here," he said. "It's a disgrace. I'm trying to make a living, and these young kids are robbing me blind." He paused for a moment. "I should think so," he said. "I was about to call the police." He hung up the phone and turned to me.

"Your father is coming," he said.

fifteen

My father surprised me. He looked imposing, like a parent, and he had dressed for the occasion. No schleppy jeans and T-shirt; he'd put on real trousers and a button-down shirt. He walked straight to the back of the pharmacy and said a few words to the man in the white coat. We sat primly, we three girls, in the chairs set up for old people waiting for their prescriptions.

"I'm sorry," my father was saying over his shoulder, as he gestured for us to leave.

"Thank you," said the pharmacist, the other parent, head cocked as he watched us leave the store.

My father led us to the car and unlocked the rear door. The three of us piled in, ready for our punishment. No one wanted to sit next to him in the front seat.

"Where can I drop you, Angie?"

"Home, I guess."

"Zoe, are you going with her?"

"No," I said, glancing sideways at Rachel. "I'll come home with you."

We stopped in front of Angie's, and I said I'd call her.

The Cohen sisters were alone with their father. I waited for him to speak.

"Rachel, your mother is going to be very disappointed in you."

"I know," said Rachel in a small voice.

And that was it. He didn't say another word. I looked at the back of my father's head, at the bald patch with the short skimpy strands of hair around it, and I hated him. Because I knew, deep in my heart, that if my father hadn't become sick, Rachel never would have done this.

When we got home, Rachel went straight to her room, and I went to mine. Cara, as usual, wasn't home. I would talk to her later about Rachel. I opened up my desk drawer and pulled out my poetry folder and an empty sheet of paper. The house was quiet. I could hear the ticking of my alarm clock. I stared at my paper. Then I wrote:

> There's a stigma around,
> Free-floating, unfair.
> It clings to my skin
> and it nests in my hair.
> It slices quite thinly
> in New York, in Yonkers.
> It cuts to the quick
> if your father is bonkers.

I laughed out loud at the ending and clapped my hand across my mouth. Then I put the sheet of paper at the bottom of the folder and rifled through the poems for one about springtime. I drew a star on it and wrote on top, in Magic Marker: "Mr. Shapiro—For publication." Maybe I would show him the rest. Maybe I wouldn't. He might think I was nuts.

My mother came into the house humming. She'd been doing that, like she was happy when she was away, and then she'd cross the threshold and the humming would stop. I could hear her come in, books thrown on the table, calling, "Ben?" My father must have answered, because she started talking, and then I heard her say "What?" followed by "Oh, for God's sake." That's when I went downstairs.

My mother was sitting at the dining room table with her head in her hands, and that scared me. My mother was the rock, and rocks are not supposed to crumble. My father stood next to her and gave me a mournful little smile as I came in.

"Mom," I said, and she looked up at me. "It was only a lipstick," I said feebly.

She just shook her head ever so slightly, in a kind of tremor, like Uncle Sol with his Parkinson's disease. "That's it," she said finally.

I sat down across from her. "Do you want me to make you some coffee?" I said.

She turned her lips up in a smile that was more like a grimace. "It's not your problem," said my mother.

"She's my sister," I said, picking at the straw place mat in front of me.

"You'll ruin that mat," said my mother, and then: "I'm sorry. . . . You're right. You're a part of this family." She turned her head and strained to look up at my father. "What are we going to do, Ben?" she said wearily.

My father pressed his lips together. "We'll think of something," he answered.

My mother narrowed her eyes at him and said, "We will?" Then she gathered her books and stood up. "We will?" she shouted at him, and she left the room.

I wandered back upstairs and stood in front of Rachel's

closed door. It was a full minute before I knocked. "What?" said Rachel, short and sharp.

"It's me," I said feebly.

She didn't answer.

"I just want to talk to you," I said. I turned the doorknob, half waiting for a shoe to hit the door like in those Divorce Italian Style movies, where the people throw things at each other when they're mad. I pushed the door open.

Rachel was lying down, her face to the wall. She didn't tell me to leave. Even so, I didn't sit beside her. I perched, Indian-fashion, next to her bed, on the throw rug shaped like a lamb.

"I know you must be feeling bad," I said to her chubby backside. There was something about its shape that made me teary. She didn't answer.

"It's not an easy time," I said stupidly, like I was talking about the Vietnam War or something.

I tried once more. "I mean, I'm having a hard time too."

She stirred a little. "You are?" she said, her voice muffled behind a hand.

"Definitely," I said, encouraged.

"How?"

How? I thought. "With boys and stuff."

"Oh," she said. "That."

She dismissed me, I know she did, but I bumbled on. "If you need to talk or anything, I'm here for you. I'm your sister." I didn't know what else to say. It wasn't juvenile delinquency. One lipstick did not make it a federal case.

"Life stinks," said Rachel.

"I know." I really couldn't argue with her. "Maybe we can help each other." I touched her back, rubbed it like she needed a massage. She moved her head toward me ever so slightly.

"Everybody else seems to be doing so . . ." She turned

her head back to the wall, searched for her word. ". . . good. Like they're having a great time or something."

"I don't really think they are," I said, adding, "Dad's not."

Rachel snorted, but she moved to sit up. She curled her legs up and swiveled around, facing me.

"Mom's not, either," I said. There was a knock on the door, and I jumped guiltily.

"Can I come in?" said my mother, entering without waiting for an answer. She looked at me. "Could I talk to your sister alone?" she said.

I got up to leave.

"I want her to stay," said Rachel.

I looked at my mother, and she shrugged her permission.

My mother sat on the bed next to Rachel, and I took my former position on the floor.

Lillian Cohen turned professor right away. "I know you're sorry you stole the lipstick, Rachel."

"I am?" said Rachel defiantly. I shrank back.

"If you're not, you should be," said my mother sharply. She sighed. Lately, it seems, my mother sighs more than she talks. "Don't ever do that again, Rachel. If you need a lipstick, I'll buy you one."

"I didn't need a lipstick," said my sister. "I don't even wear lipstick."

"Then why?" said my mother.

"Because I wanted to."

I looked at my mother's eyes. They had dark rings around them, as if someone had smudged them with sepia pastel. "I'll try to get you some help, Rachel," she said.

It was like I was watching a play, with the two of them sitting on my sister's bed. Rachel's eyes were brimming with tears now. "What do you mean?" she said.

"A therapist, someone to talk to," said my mother, reaching out to wipe the single tear that rolled down Rachel's cheek.

Rachel pulled back, and my play turned into a baseball game. One strike. Two strikes. Three strikes, you're out, and you join my father on the bench—or should I say, on the psychiatrist's couch.

"I know the family is suffering," said my mother, her eyes darting down to the floor so that her middle child could be included in the understatement of the year.

"I'm just trying to pay the bills and keep the family together," my mother continued in her world-weary voice. "If this keeps up, I'll have to teach some classes in the evening."

The Cohen sisters were quiet.

My mother picked up Rachel's limp hand and squeezed it. "We'll look back at all this someday and laugh," she said, but I've never seen two faces further from laughter.

Mom sat forward and pushed herself off the bed. She stood up and plucked at a wrinkle in her skirt, then she rested her hand on the top of my head. "We'll get through this," she whispered, and I was sorry when she took her hand away.

"Dinner will be ready in an hour or so," she said over her shoulder.

I stood up and waited until I could hear her footsteps on the stairs. "Maybe it would help to talk to someone," I said to Rachel.

"Then *you* talk."

"Maybe I will," I said, losing my big-sister cool. Let Cara deal with her, the ungrateful bitch.

Maybe I would give Oprah Winfrey a call and suggest a new topic: "Children of Depression."

Cara was no help at all. As I wandered downstairs to help with dinner, I heard noises coming from the basement. Happy noises, like laughter, so I knew it wasn't my father.

"Who's that?" I asked, putting the forks on the right, defiantly.

My mother didn't correct me. "Cara and Billy. I told her he could stay until supper if she did the washing up."

"You didn't invite him?"

"There isn't enough." My mother snapped string beans into a bowl. "I'm not Lady Bountiful."

Witch. I finished setting the table and opened the basement door. More laughter. I bounded noisily down the stairs in case I was interrupting any funny business, even though I could no longer call whatever went on between the sexes funny. Cara was sprawled across the old couch, and Billy was tickling her into torrents of laughter. "Say uncle," he said, torturing her under the armpit with an index finger.

"Aunt," gasped Cara, pulling her legs up and clamping her arms against her sides.

"Say uncle," continued Billy, tossing a smile at me, going for her stomach.

"Never," screeched Cara. "Aunt, aunt."

Billy put a hand on his hip and turned to me in mock exasperation. "Are you a feminist like your sister? Am I allowed to say 'sister,' or do I have to say 'sibling'?"

Cara sat up almost primly, a smile still on her face. "What's up?" she said to me.

"Did you hear about Rachel?"

"Briefly. Mom told me. What about it?"

"What about it? Mom's sending her to a shrink."

"Good," said Cara. "Maybe he'll put her on a diet too."

"You don't sound very concerned."

Cara shrugged. "There isn't much I can do." She reached out for Billy's hand and pulled him down on the couch.

Billy circled a biceps over her shoulder. "We care," he said. "You guys are getting the fallout."

I could have punched him in the nose. "Fallout? What do you think this is, a nuclear war?"

"From the depression. The bomb's gone off, and you're experiencing the aftermath."

"What aftermath?" I wanted to prove him wrong, dead wrong, Dr. Jock Freud. "What bomb? A bomb I would notice. There's nothing. My dad doesn't show anything. He brought Rachel home and told her how disappointed her mother would be. Her mother! What about him?"

"He's too busy trying to keep his head above water."

Cara smiled proudly at her man. "He's been reading up. Real case histories."

"Oh, bully."

"It's Billy." He smiled at me, a winning jock smile. "Billy's the name, not bully."

It was wasted on me. Cara noticed. "Hey, lighten up, will you?"

"Did you tell her about Sam?" Billy caressed one of Cara's shoulders, kind of like he owned her, like any move he made would be welcomed by her. I was jealous. Not of Billy; he wasn't my type. But of the ease of it all.

I could feel my bulldog frown. "Who's Sam?" I said testily.

"Sam Prelutsky. A buddy of mine. He thinks you're cute."

"God only knows why! Look at the face on her!" Cara was pissed at me, but she softened. "We thought maybe we could all go out together someday."

"I'm not into blind dates," I said.

I turned to go up the stairs, hoping for a reprieve. Try it, you might like it, or something like that.

"Suit yourself," Billy called after me.

"He deserves better," added Cara.

My father was sitting at the table, eating his salad.

"Dad couldn't wait," said my mother from the kitchen, excusing him.

I sat down next to him, leaned my chin on my hand, and watched him. He was eating mechanically, kind of shoveling the lettuce into his mouth with great precision. Hunger didn't seem to enter into it.

I picked up my fork and joined him. When we'd finished, he sat mutely, expectantly, like the old folks in Uncle Sol's nursing home, who gathered in the dining room an hour before supper, waiting for the main event of the day.

"Is the psychiatrist helping you?" I said. No intro. No warning. I wondered if my mother was listening in the kitchen. She didn't swoop in and rescue him, so I pressed forward. "Are you getting better?"

My father looked surprised. He cocked his head to the side and said, "I don't think so. It doesn't feel like it."

I was stunned. Why couldn't he lie, like he did when my mother came home with a bad haircut, short and shaved, and he told her how beautiful she looked. Later, he whispered to me, "They're trying to turn her into a militant feminist."

He picked up a fork and traced a pattern on the white tablecloth. The fork left faint marks on the fabric. He was mesmerized, much more interested in them than in me.

"The guy in the Hitchcock picture did that," I said. "Gregory Peck."

He looked up. "The one where the airplane chases him?"

"No, that's Cary Grant," I corrected him. My father used to know much more about the movies than I did.

"The one about the loony bin!" Brightness came into his eyes, and he started to laugh. "Very fitting," he said, gasping. He shook with laughter until I could see little tears squeeze their way out of his eyes. "Doesn't he turn out to be a murderer?" he said, sputtering into another spasm of laughter.

"He goes off with his shrink, Ingrid Bergman."

My father's laughter was hysterical now. "That's what I'll do," he said, holding his stomach. "I'll run off with Dr. Grubman. Herbert and I will run off together."

"Like in *Casablanca*," I said.

"The beginning of a beautiful friendship," said my father.

My mother entered the dining room with a platter of chicken. "What's so funny?" she asked cautiously. She seemed pleased, though, because she came up behind my father and put her arms around him.

"Herbert and me, Lil. The match of the century."

"What on earth are you talking about?" said my mother.

"Movie talk," I said, watching her kiss him on the ear.

"Looney tunes," said my father as she released him.

That evening, Angie called to check up on me.

"Margot invited us to a party tonight."

"Oh God," I said.

"I know, but it could be fun."

"Spare me."

"Come on, you're an experienced woman now."

"I'm experienced enough to kill myself."

"Don't do that," said my friend.

"Go with Margot," I said. "I want to stay home with my looney-tune family." I echoed my father, but I didn't want Angie to agree with me.

"I stole stuff when I was young. It's normal."

"Like what?"

"Oh, the odd piece of bubble gum."

"Big deal."

"A lipstick is nothing."

"My mother is sending her to a shrink." I waited for Angie to confirm my suspicions, that my whole family was nuts.

"Rachel's fine," said Angie. "It's a hard age."

"Go to the party," I said. "I have a feeling tonight's the night."

"Then I'd better go."

"Goodbye, Petal," I said to her.

"Goodbye, rat."

I went to bed early. Some nights I'd watch the eleven o'clock news with my parents. My father would comment on the girth of Barbara Bush. My mother would chide him: "She's a lot more human than Nancy Reagan. Her I hated like poison." Then my father would laugh.

I always wear a nightgown. Cara sleeps in the raw. More liberated than I am, I guess. Tonight, I just slipped off my underwear and slid into bed, felt the relief of being encased in softness, the weight of the cover. I tucked it around me, right up to my chin. I touched my breasts, tested them for firmness, but lying on my back, they virtually disappeared into the bone. My stomach was flat, thank God. I hadn't done the ruler test in a while. Lying down, you lay a ruler across your hipbones, and if the mound of your stomach touches the ruler, you're fat. Rachel would fail. My hand moved cautiously. I knew I wouldn't go blind if I touched myself down there, but it didn't feel natural. It felt sinful, which didn't make any sense, because Catholics are supposed to feel guilty about stuff like that, not Jews. I touched myself gingerly, and felt a stirring that I didn't feel with Richie. I played lightly, gently tapping myself—good girl, good girl— until I found a rhythm that I didn't want to stop playing, so I played it to the end, when I hit a rousing finale that overwhelmed me with its fierceness, and I hardly knew it was me. At least I knew I wasn't frigid.

sixteen

Mr. Shapiro skimmed his hand in a backward swoop over the top of his head. There was no hair to ruffle, just a smooth pink egg of a head that shone like the legs of the sun-worshipers at the pool club. As if he rubbed baby oil on it every night. My father's baldness was different, less tidy, with wisps of hair everywhere, so that he kept it short and military. Mr. Shapiro's was movie-star baldness. Yul Brynner. He reveled in it. Now he was licking his lips, his tongue a little minnow darting about on the lower part of his mouth as a signal that serious talk was about to occur.

"I've called you in today—" he began.

"I'm just reading through a batch of stuff I collected yesterday," I interrupted.

"Don't worry about that," he said, waving his hand in the air. "I want to talk about you."

Who? Who? I intoned in my head, an owl about to have a heart attack as he pulled out my folder of poetry. Why had I submitted everything?

"I like some of this a lot," he said, sifting through the papers.

But? But?

"But you sound troubled, Zoe."

Me? Me? I felt myself shrinking back. I couldn't help him, couldn't clear up matters for him with a recitation of what was wrong with my life.

"Is there anything you'd like to talk about?" Mr. Shapiro was leaning toward me now, his smooth egghead close to me, the earnest look in his eyes pushing me away fast.

I shrugged my shoulders, Rachel-style.

But Mr. Shapiro continued on his mission, pulling out the poem about my father going bonkers. "Your father seems to figure in much of this."

I shrugged again, but a spring of water was gathering behind my eyes. I blinked to keep it back.

"Is he sick?"

"He's sick, all right," I blurted out. Traitor.

"Physically?" Mr. Shapiro's voice was gentle.

By now I knew that the twenty questions wouldn't stop. "He's . . . depressed." I was sick of the word, sick of feeling ashamed, sick of not knowing how to explain it.

"I see." The egghead moved away from me.

How *could* he see?

"I mean . . . I know what you're going through." He scratched an eyebrow, the only hair on his body, from the looks of it. "My wife suffers from depression." He blinked his eyes.

It was my turn to see. I had joined his club. People who lived with nutcases should stick together.

"It's very, very hard," he said, "because it seems like such a . . ." He paused. I waited. ". . . a selfish disease. You feel like he's not there for you."

"He isn't," I said.

"I know. He's gone. But he'll come back. My wife is fine

127

now. I have my wife back, just like your father will get better too. Is he in treatment?"

I gave him a half nod, half shrug, shifted in my seat like he was giving a lecture on something boring like Beowulf.

"Look . . . if you'd like to talk, I'm always here." Mr. Shapiro turned businesslike and picked up a pencil, ready to correct papers or something. "Or you can always talk to the guidance counselor, Mrs. Chain."

It was a bad name for a guidance counselor; the kids all called her Mrs. Chainsaw Massacre. I stood up and metamorphosed into the polite kid my parents raised. "Thanks a lot, Mr. Shapiro," I said.

"I mean it, Zoe."

"Thanks," I said again, pushing back my chair and heading for the door.

"One more thing, Zoe."

I turned.

"The poems about your father are excellent."

I smiled and walked out of the room, though it felt like I was bursting out of a vacuum-packed can. I wasn't used to it at all—a man talking to me like he was really interested. A man talking to me like his next move wasn't to put his hand down my shirt.

So who do I bump into? A Roman god who will never be interested in putting his hand anywhere, but Alex stops, and looks me in the eye, and hands me a piece of paper, folded small.

"For you," he says, and maybe I look startled, because his face breaks into a grin. "For the magazine."

So it wasn't a declaration of undying love, a missive celebrating my round hips and glorious hair. I waited until he rounded the corner, unfolded the paper, and read it.

Life's just a bowlful of cherries—
That's what the people say.
Every cloud has a silver lining.
All they want is a roll in the hay.
But I have another theory,
For the guys who like bodies and legs:
Life's not a bowlful of cherries,
It's a carton of one dozen eggs.
Some of them make a good pie crust.
Some of them dye up real pink.
Some of them scramble for breakfast.
And some of them basically stink.
But maybe I'm talking too quickly.
Maybe the cherry part fits—
If life is a bowlful of cherries,
How come I keep getting the pits?

I refolded the piece of paper like a car map that my mother insists be closed perfectly, the picture on the front. It occurred to me that the poem would give me a chance to talk to Alex. But what would I say? I wondered if the dozen eggs were girls. And was Lynn Baker a rotten one, or one that made good pie crust, or a cherry pit? I wasn't ready for Alex, who was leaning against the fence when I walked out the door.

"Well?" He had the same grin on his face, a grin that said, You're one of the eggs, and I can scramble you if I want.

"It's funny," I said.

"And?"

"You don't usually make pie crust out of eggs."

Alex laughed. "What can I tell you? It rhymed."

By now we were walking together, and my heart was doing its usual Roman-god dance. "Do you really keep getting the pits?" I said.

"Sure. I just spit them out!"

"So what kind of egg am I?" I said, throwing caution to the winds.

"Who knows?" said Alex mysteriously. "I haven't cracked you open yet."

"Maybe I make a good French toast," I said, appalled at my bravery.

But Alex seemed to like it. "With sugar or syrup?" he said, rubbing my arm.

"Syrup," I said in my creamiest tone. I was making myself a little nauseous.

"Want to meet me at Grumpy John's on Friday?"

I filled my voice with the biggest dose of syrup and honey and brown sugar that I could muster, even though I could hear Angie whisper in my ear, Don't sound too eager. "I'd love to," I said.

By Friday night, I was a basket case, but a happy one. I wore my favorite slouchy sweater and tight black pants, and my dad actually told me how pretty I looked. Cara helped me put on my makeup and didn't even get mad when I ve-toed the lip pencil because it made me look like Bozo the clown.

"Suit yourself," she said, stepping back to admire her handi-work.

Angie called to give me last-minute advice. "I heard my mother tell her friend that men like a slut in bed and a lady in public."

"There are no beds at Grumpy John's, and if we go any-where near the river, I'll jump in."

Angie laughed. "Just play it cool, and you'll do fine."

It's hard to play it cool when you're sweating, but as I walked to Grumpy John's, I tried to talk the butterflies out of my stomach. I was too hot in the sweater, with my jean jacket on top, but when I took a last look in my pocket mirror, the flush on my face made me look kind of pretty.

He was there when I arrived, and I sat down opposite him. It felt almost like an audition for a summer job: yes, I can do it; yes, I'll take any salary you offer; yes, I'm the best person for the position; like me, like me, please like me.

"You don't like pepperoni, do you?" That was his opening line.

"No," I said, hoping that I wasn't immediately relegated to the nerd category.

"I ordered us a plain pizza."

"Great," I said. It was weird being able to look directly at his face. His eyes were deeper and bluer than I remembered. It looked like he was already shaving.

Alex got up from his seat. For a moment, I pictured him walking out the door—goodbye, lady, you're boring me to death—but he went over to the refrigerator case and extracted a couple of cans of regular soda, not diet. I didn't tell him I only drank sugar-free. I hoped he couldn't tell that my legs were beginning to tremble.

"A couple of months until summer," I said. I guess sweating in my sweater reminded me of that brilliant fact, but Alex just nodded and said, "I'll be helping out at my uncle's gas station."

"I have to get a job too. My parents want me to put away some money for college."

"I forgot you're a college girl."

My heart sank a little. Because I didn't know he wasn't. A college boy, that is. And working at a gas station? Not a bank or a lawyer's office. Pumping gas. I could already hear myself defending him to my mother. I'm going out with him—I'm not marrying him.

"I want to make enough money to buy a house." At least

he's responsible, I'd tell my mother. At least he's saving his money.

Grumpy John threw a pizza on the table, and Alex took a piece.

"We lived in an apartment when I was little. A house is nice," I heard myself say. A house? I hated cleaning my own room. What would anyone want with a house? I watched Alex fold the slice of pizza in half and finish it in record time. Girls didn't eat that way. I took a bite of pizza and burned the top of my mouth. A swig of cola helped, and I wondered if Lynn Baker drank regular soda instead of diet and if her legs shook uncontrollably, like mine, underneath the table.

"So you're not going to go to college?" I said, ready for his answer, so that I could accept the fact that despite his eyes and his arms, he wasn't perfect for me. It didn't stop my legs from shaking.

Alex raised an eyebrow. "Maybe a course or two, if I feel like it. At the junior college."

"I have no idea what I want to be when I grow up," I said, as if it were a joke instead of the truth.

"I thought you liked to write. Couldn't you be a journalist or something?" Alex started on his second piece of pizza.

I heard my stomach rumble, and I took another bite. "I don't think so. Politics aren't my strong point."

"So maybe you could write a best-seller."

"I don't think I'd know what to write about."

"Sex," Alex said. "Sex sells."

"Mr. Shapiro says it's best in the beginning to write about what you know." The minute it was out, I felt my face turn bright red.

Alex laughed so loud that Grumpy John looked over. "I could give you some pointers," he said. "You're funny."

Funny was okay. I changed the subject anyway. "Angie wants to be a vet," I said. Did he remember that we were sort of talking about careers?

"What's a vet?" Alex looked at me blankly.

"A veterinarian. She loves animals."

"Oh. I had her in Vietnam or something." Alex went for his third slice of pizza.

"Angie's mother wants her to be a nurse, but Angie says she likes animals better than people." Why on earth was I talking so much about Angie?

"Cute. Is she going with anyone?"

Great. He's interested in Angie. Keep talking about her, jerk. It's *you* he asked out, I told myself. "Nobody," I said to him. "I can't understand why not." I became Angie's best friend again. "I think she's adorable."

"I heard about your lezzie activities," he said. There was a piece of tomato stuck to his lip. Even a Roman god looks lousy with a piece of tomato stuck to his lip.

"Have you heard that I'm a nymphomaniac too?" Inside, I winced. He thinks I'm funny, he thinks I'm a lesbian, and now he'll think I'm a nutcase.

Alex didn't seem to mind. "Now, *that* would be something to write about, Zoe."

It was the first time I could remember that he used my name. I longed for "darling" or "sweetheart" or "honey" or—let's face it—"my love." Even though that piece of tomato was stuck to his lip.

I started to say something, but a string of mozzarella hung out of my mouth. Peeling it as gracefully as possible off my chin, I ate it.

"Did you ever see the *I Love Lucy* show where the spaghetti is hanging out of her mouth and Ethel pulls out a pair of scissors and cuts it?" I started laughing. Call it nerves, first-date jitters, I don't know, but I couldn't stop.

"No," said Alex, raising an eyebrow and twirling a finger by his forehead like I was a crazy woman.

I stopped laughing. My worst fears had come true. He thought I was funny, a lesbian, and a total nutcase. I saw myself behind bars in a loony bin, with my father as cellmate.

"Want to get going?" Alex stood up and didn't wait for an answer.

I followed him out the door. Needless to say, I didn't tell him that if you handed the cans in at the counter, they would recycle them. And I didn't tell him about the tomato still stuck to his lip.

We walked side by side. I kept my hand available, but who would take the hand of a nutcase? A kind of darkness had descended on me, and I wondered if this was the way my father felt. I tried to shake myself out of it. Nobody likes a grouch, my mother used to tell me when Cara made fun of my bad moods, but somehow this felt much worse than grouchiness. It felt permanent.

We were heading for the war memorial. Lots of the kids hung out there on the benches, by the statue of some hero named William East, who they named our town, Eastfield, after.

Lynn Baker was sitting on the armrest of one of the benches. Casual. Confident. No jacket, like it was summer already. Boobs hanging out. Margot was there too, with Jimmy. That left Lynn on her own.

"Hey, Alex," said Jimmy, slouching toward us with his

arm around Margot. "Hey," he directed toward me, but I was nameless.

"Hi, Zoe." Margot gave me a name. "Nice new makeup!" She messed up with the makeup remark, because Alex would know how hard I had worked at looking nice for him. And that I cared.

Out of the corner of my eye, I could see Lynn drifting over. Maybe Alex saw too, because inexplicably, he took my hand. I felt like I'd been thrown a net.

"Alex, my love, you have something on your lip," Lynn said to him. "Naughty, naughty," she added, even though it was clearly a piece of food and pretty gross.

I dug in my pocket for a tissue, but I was too late. Lynn had already picked it off and wiped it ever so discreetly on the statue of William East. I could have cursed myself. The tomato was hers.

But Alex wasn't. I gave his hand a swing so that she'd notice.

Lynn pounced. "I left my earrings at your house the other day," she said.

"I'll give them to you at school on Monday," Alex said.

"They were on the coffee table by the couch." Lynn gave me a look that truckdrivers usually give you when you're walking down the street, except she didn't whistle apprecia-tively, she just moved her eyes up and down. And maybe I was being paranoid again, but she looked like she was about to snarl. I gave Alex's hand a second little swing.

"We were at Grumpy John's," I said to Margot.

"Come to Gary's with us," she said. "His parents are out."

Alex pulled me toward him and said, "Sounds good to me." As he led me away, I wondered vaguely why I hadn't been able to tell him that I didn't really want to go to Gary's house, that I preferred sugar-free soda, that I thought college was pretty important, that I wasn't crazy, that not everybody can write a best-seller, and especially, most important of all, that he was wearing a piece of tomato on his lip, and that I, Zoe Cohen, was capable of removing it.

I don't remember much of Gary's house, because we only saw the basement. I had caught a glimpse of some red velvet couches covered in plastic, which my parents wouldn't be caught dead owning, much less covering in Saran wrap. Then we turned the corner into the kitchen, and I saw a little wooden magnet on the refrigerator, marked "Carol's Kitchen." I would have liked to examine the refrigerator some more—my father once said that you can figure out a family by what they put on the door: drawings, bills, notes. But we headed downstairs.

A few boys were playing pool. Alex and Jimmy immediately joined them, so Margot and I headed for an ugly brown couch, where a couple of girls I'd never seen before were sitting. Lynn stood by the boys, jutting out one limb or another and watching the pool playing like it was the seventh game in the World Series. She made Margot look like an amateur.

Margot squeezed next to me on the couch. "So?" she breathed in my ear. "When did they break up?"

"I didn't ask him." Lynn was leaning on Alex now, and I sat forward.

"As long as she's not after Jimmy anymore." Margot must have seen my stricken look, because she said quickly, "Relax. She's looking desperate."

She didn't look desperate to me. She was laughing so hard I caught a glimpse of her tonsils. "What do you think I should do?" I said to Margot.

"Watch me," said Margot. She stood up and stretched. "Hey, Jimmy," she called.

Round Two: Margot struts her stuff. Jimmy turned, said a few words to the other boys, and left his pool stick on the table.

Margot held out her arms to him, and he gave her a kiss that looked so wet I thought I saw saliva dribbling down the side of his mouth.

But it worked. Alex disengaged himself, left his pool stick, and like a twin brother to Jimmy, gave me his tomato-free mouth. And this time, I liked it.

At least I thought I did, until Jimmy grabbed Margot's hand and started pulling her up the stairs. I know, because my eyes were open while I checked out Margot's technique. Alex's eyes must have been open too, because he stopped kissing me and said, "Good idea." My heart started hammering as he led me up the linoleum stairs, up a set of carpeted stairs, down a carpeted hallway, and into what must have been the parents' bedroom, because the bed was enormous and flowered, and it was covered with pillows that didn't look like Gary's taste.

I lay down on the big bed and kept my eyes glued to a blue pillow with hieroglyphics on it, kind of mesmerizing myself as Alex kissed my neck and shoulders and ears, wondering if this was the way it was supposed to feel, and did Gary's father have a bad back, because the mattress was so much harder than my parents' bed, and would I be thinking these things if I was really a passionate person?

And then all I could think about was Richie, and how I couldn't say no to him, and if I couldn't say no to someone I wasn't even sure I liked, how could I say no to somebody I did? Alex was kissing me some more, and I watched as his hand traveled across a flowered sham and past my blue hieroglyphic pillow and brushed along my side and up under my sweater in the same familiar dance that John did and Richie did, and I wondered if Lycra stretch pants would work as well as reinforced panty hose, because my brain wasn't signaling my mouth to say No No No No No.

I heard ringing in my ears, a persistent ringing, and then the bedroom door opened and Alex sprang off the bed as I yanked my sweater down and I heard Alex say, "What's going on?" and I heard somebody say, "The police," but it wasn't the police, it was Gary's parents, and it was Carol of Carol's Kitchen who was ringing the doorbell, because her husband was putting the car in the garage and she didn't have her key. I barreled down the stairs and past a lady with frosted hair who must have been Carol and heard myself say hello to her like I had my mother inside my head telling me to be polite, but I was gone before she could even answer.

s e v e n t e e n

Margot was pretty nice," I said, telling Angie about the dynamic kissing duo she had initiated.

"She has a good heart," said Angie, sounding doubtful even as she said it. Then she added, "She just spreads it around a little."

Angie and I were stretched out on my parents' bed. We sometimes did that when we wanted to talk privately, with my mother at work and my father downstairs vacuuming.

"I'll never hear from him again," I told Angie. "He kissed me good night at the door and didn't say a word about seeing him again. 'Bye.' That's all he said. He hates me." I waited for Angie, my best friend, to protest.

She didn't disappoint me. " 'Bye' means goodbye, dope. That's all."

I knew Angie meant it, she really did. But I also knew that she always says I look fine, even when I've gained five pounds and my hips are draping over my pants. I tried to shake her faith in me. "He could have said, 'I'll call you.' "

Angie snorted. "My cousin says *that's* what they say when they *never* plan on calling you."

"And they say 'Bye' when they've had the worst evening in their lives."

"I'm not talking to you." Angie rolled over on her stomach and buried her head in the pillow. "You went out with Alex," she said in a muffled voice, "and now all I get are complaints." She turned her head so that I could see her profile. "What about me?" she said. "How come nobody's asking *me* out?"

"I told Alex you were adorable," I said meekly.

"Big deal. He probably thinks I'm a dog." Angie rolled over again and gave me an accusing look. "So are we going into the city tomorrow and staying over at your grandma's or not?"

"What if he calls?" The minute it was out, I knew I was in trouble.

Angie glared at me. "Are you the type who dumps her girlfriend when a boy asks her out?"

"Only sometimes," I said, meek as a mouse again. "You want the truth, don't you? I drank regular soda for this guy. I didn't even tell him there was tomato on his mouth, because I was afraid I'd insult him. I'm a weakling."

There was a knock on the door, and my father entered. "I just have to get a sweater," he said. "Your mother asked me to do some shopping."

"Hi, Mr. Cohen," said Angie, sitting up like it was more proper that way.

"Hi, Angie." I was glad he could remember her name.

My father opened the closet door and took an old sweater off a hook. Sticking out of the hanging shoe rack was a battered pair of moccasins that he loved to wear in the garden— B.C., of course. Before crisis, when he took an interest in things like gardening. The wooden box that contained all my father's shoe-polishing paraphernalia stood on the floor. B.C., my father used to sit on sheets of newspaper, fiddle with the radio for a station, and polish all our shoes. The twang of country and western music would fill the air, and my mother would yell, "What's that rubbish doing on?" "That's shoe-polishing music, Lil," my father would answer. Then he'd laugh, like he was some little kid who had gotten away with murder.

He put on his sweater and reiterated, "I'm going to do a little shopping for your mother." I could see the list now. She had to write down every little detail—the brand, the exact size to the ounce—or he'd come home with the smallest size laundry detergent and the dinkiest jar of mayonnaise. She couldn't even write "salad stuff," because he didn't know what it meant. Lettuce. Tomato. Cucumber. Mushrooms. He ate salad every night at supper, but my mother had to spell out every item.

My father left the room. I was glad when Angie didn't say anything.

"We'll go into the city tomorrow," I told her. Stay home all day with my father, like some puppet, waiting for a phone call? No way.

At the station the next day, Angie gave me the bad news. It's not that I don't like Margot. I do. But when Angie told me she was coming with us, I groaned.

"I couldn't help it. I told her what we were doing, and she took me by surprise," said Angie.

"She can't sleep over at my grandma's. There's no room."

"I told her." Angie said in a low voice, "Be quiet. Here she is."

Margot took over the train station. She ripped open a packet of gum, settled her pocketbook on the bench, laughed out loud at a piece of graffiti on the wall, poked her head inside the bathroom door and emerged feigning strangulation—all minor stuff, performance art, but everybody was watching.

"Let's go to the Village. I want to buy a pair of earrings. Or an ankle bracelet." Now Margot was planning our day for us. The train pulled into the station, and we followed Margot down the aisle, to the seat of her choice.

The crowds and the hustle at Penn Station cheered me up. I tried not to look at the homeless people scattered around the station like abandoned mannequins, except when one of them lifted up a bottle and drank, or held out a hand. A man who looked like an unkempt Jesus Christ stood up and slouched over to Margot and touched her sleeve. His hand was etched with dirt.

"Do you have a match?" he mumbled, holding out the butt of a cigarette with the other grubby hand.

Walk away, I thought, he'll grab your purse, he'll stick you with a dirty needle, but Margot stood her ground and fished in her pocketbook. "Keep it," she said, throwing him a book of matches. It landed on the floor, and the man had to stoop down and pick it up. He groaned like my grandmother did with her arthritis.

"Let's get out of here," said Angie, grabbing Margot's hand and dragging her along while I ran beside them.

Margot laughed. "That could be me someday," she said, throwing off Angie's hand and pointing toward the exit. "That-away," she said.

We walked over to Fifth Avenue and headed downtown. It was a beautiful spring day, and since Angie and I didn't have much money, we peered in lots of plate-glass windows. We passed a couple of restaurants, and Margot said, "Let's go in for a drink." Angie vetoed it before I did. Sometimes

Margot would wave to a cute waiter, and they always seemed to wave back. I tried to picture myself waving, but I knew that Margot could get away with it, Lynn Baker could get away with it, but not Zoe Cohen. They'd sniff me out, they'd smell *small town* on me, they'd know I was from New Jersey.

We could see the Washington Square arch now, and I felt like I was in Paris or something. I squeezed Angie's hand, and she squeezed back. Angie never made me feel like a nerd. Margot spotted a Good Humor truck, and we bought toasted-almond bars and walked into the park.

Margot sat down on a bench next to an old man and said, "Can we join you?"

The man looked kind of dazed, but he nodded, and Margot moved closer to him to make room for us. I think she bounced around too much, because he got up and left.

"Good," said Margot, like she'd organized his departure. "We have the bench to ourselves."

We watched a tall coffee-colored man fly a kite. He ran like a graceful hunter, a dancer about to spear a moving jackrabbit on a steppe or a walkabout or whatever you call it. I know it's pretty dumb when you hear people say stuff like black people have more rhythm, but he moved like a warrior.

Maybe Margot thought so too, because she called out to him, "Nice kite," and I could have killed her. It's one thing giving out matches to a bum in the station, and it's another talking to a perfect stranger.

He started walking toward us, and she said, "Can I try?" Angie and I rolled our eyes at each other.

He was smiling widely now, dimpled, dark, a fine sweat on his forehead. He pulled a red polka-dotted neckerchief out of his pocket and wiped his face. "Be my guest," he said, handing Margot the kite. "My name is Gabriel."

"I'm Margot, and this is Angie and Zoe." Margot took

hold of the string and went running, which was no mean feat, because there were so many people in the park that she had to skirt around them. Her breasts took on a rhythm of their own, and I watched Gabriel watch Margot's dancing twin bongos. I poked Angie in the side with my elbow, and she poked me back, and we sat there, disapproving spinster aunts with our elbows digging into each other.

When Margot was finished, she ran back to us, flushed in the face and panting. Gabriel held out the same red polka-dot neckerchief and she took it, dabbing at her forehead and the top of her breasts. I sucked in some air, suppressing the word "cooties." Don't get me wrong—it wasn't because he was black but because he was an unknown quantity, and Margot was acting like she'd known him forever.

He offered us peppermints from a crumpled white bag, the red-and-white-striped kind that you see around Christmas, and we two Goody Two-shoes shook our heads—never accept candy from strangers—but Margot reached inside the bag and took two of them. "One for the train ride home," she said. We were sitting on the bench, three white girls and a kite-flying stranger, until Margot stood up and said, "I'm sweating." She sat down on the grass behind the bench, and Gabriel joined her.

By the time I turned around to look, he had his arm around her.

"What do you do besides flying kites?" I heard Margot ask him.

"I'm a playwriter," said the man, in a lilting voice.

I hissed at Angie, "If he's really a playwright, don't you think he'd know the right word for it?"

"I can't believe this," Angie hissed back.

We waited a few minutes and got up off the bench, trying

to look nonchalant as we turned to find out what Margot was up to.

They were lying on the grass, mouths jammed together in a kind of lockjaw. The kite was getting squashed, but neither of them seemed to notice.

"Goodbye, Margot," called Angie, the brave one, as we started to walk. Margot and the "playwriter" scrambled to their feet.

I expected Gabriel to look embarrassed, but he smiled and pulled out a kind of antique pocket watch. He consulted it and said, "Come with me and see my friend's play."

"Play what?" said Angie. "Footsie?"

Margot cracked up, but Gabriel looked injured.

"My playwriter friend," he said. "His play is on, in the East Village."

Angie and I didn't need to consult each other. We shook our heads, just as Margot uttered, "Great!"

Angie and I pulled Margot into a football huddle, and Angie muttered in Margot's ear, "Are you crazy?"

"You don't even know this guy," I whispered, with equal fierceness.

"He's a gas," said Margot. "I thought your mother was the type that liked plays and stuff."

"She wouldn't like me making out in the grass with a complete stranger," I said.

Margot turned the color of her blush-on and jutted her chin out. "I'll go with you," she said to Gabriel. He took her hand and waved to us with his free one.

Angie and I watched as the odd couple headed for the arch, the dark warrior walking on air, the blonde from New Jersey strutting her stuff.

"Why?" I said to Angie. "Why did she do it?"

Angie shrugged. "I have a theory," she said.

"Tell me, O great and wise one." I joked, but Angie is actually pretty smart.

"Her father left her mother, you know."

"So?"

"So she always has to prove herself. Over and over."

"How? By making out with total strangers?"

Angie raised an eyebrow. "By hooking any man she can get, looking for her father."

"Sounds too deep to me," I told her. But the looking-for-her-father part got me. It clanged in my head. "How'd you figure that out?" I asked.

"I watch a lot of talk shows." She laughed as she headed down the sidewalk.

We hooked arms and started chanting, "Lions and tigers and bears, oh my!" over and over, passing by our bench with the matted grass behind it. "He left his kite," I said, examining the scene of the crime.

Angie didn't say a word. She just unhooked her arm, walked over to the kite, and picked it up. It flopped, an animal with a broken back, and Angie threw it in the nearest litter basket.

Grandma gave us blintzes for supper and offered us coffee afterward, but Angie had soda and I had tea. We took out our new earrings and admired them, while Grandma got towels out of the closet.

"You'll sleep in my bed," she said. "I'll sleep on the couch."

I didn't protest, because Grandma snored, and she knew it, from when my Grandpa was alive and used to sleep with plugs in his ears.

It was weird sleeping in the same bed with Angie. There was a hollow in the middle, and we rolled into it so that our shoulders touched. We smiled at each other, and Angie turned her back to me. It was a relief being with somebody who didn't want to stick a hand up my shirt. As I drifted off, I wondered what the Jewish equivalent of a nun was.

I woke up thinking about Margot. Maybe she was the flip side of Zoe Cohen. Opinionated, outgoing, a performer. But maybe when it came to men, she was just as lost as I was. Always looking for approval. Chickenshit when it came to saying no.

The smell of Grandma's challah French toast came drifting into the bedroom, and I slipped out of bed and put on a pink fake-silk bathrobe that somebody had given Grandma.

"Take it home with you," she said when she saw it on me. Grandma set a plate of French toast in front of me and poured herself some coffee.

"So how's your poor father?" she said, putting a drop of synthetic milk into the cup. "I hate this stuff like poison," she added.

"He's the same," I said, smothering my French toast with the real maple syrup my mother had brought back from our last vacation in Vermont. I didn't have to pretend with my grandmother. "I hate him," I told her, putting a piece of toast in my mouth.

My grandmother shook her head. "You don't hate him," she said.

"I do!" I answered. "I'm sick of it. Depression! I never want to hear the word again."

"It's a terrible thing." My grandmother picked at a piece of dry roll sitting on the table.

"I'll probably inherit it."

My grandmother snorted. "You take after your mother's side of the family. We're worriers."

"Anxiety is the flip side of depression," I said, but I welcomed her idea.

"Like hell," said my grandmother. "Worriers get a lot more done."

"It's awful," I said, starting on my second piece of French toast.

"At least it doesn't affect your appetite," said Grandma, laughing. She sipped her coffee and sighed her arthritic sigh. "Maybe the new treatment will help," she said.

"What new treatment?" I put my fork down so hard that the hotel plate rang.

"Your mother didn't tell you?" My grandmother's face was veiled now.

"Tell me what?"

"For God's sake, you're almost sixteen years old. She should have told you."

I felt the French toast flop in my stomach, and I said, "If you don't tell me now, I'm going to call my mother."

My grandmother sighed again. "He's going into the hospital for some treatment," she said.

"What kind of treatment? He's already seeing a shrink."

"Electric shock therapy, I think it's called."

"You're kidding me." I watched my grandmother busy herself washing dishes. "I thought they didn't do that kind of thing anymore."

"Your mother says they do."

I felt like the breath was knocked out of me. "I thought . . ." I didn't know what I thought. "Electric shock treatment? Doesn't that kill brain cells or something? Don't you lose your memory and walk around in a fog? Like in that movie about the film star? *Frances.*"

My grandmother reached down and opened up a cabinet. "This pan needs some Brillo," she said, rummaging for the box. She pulled out a wad of steel wool and held it under the running water. "I think you're talking about a lobotomy," she said softly, scrubbing the frying pan. With the water running, I could barely hear her. "Your father isn't getting one of those," she said. She turned and looked at me. "I can never get this pan clean," she said.

Angie padded into the kitchen, and Grandma clammed up and did her hostess bit, offering her everything in the refrigerator from eggs to blintzes. I could tell she was horrified when Angie settled for a glass of cream soda.

We took the subway to Penn Station and waited for our train. I was glad that Angie was as quiet as I was, because by now I was picturing hospitals with prison bars and straitjackets and my father lying on a white table with wires coming out of his ears. Maybe Angie was thinking about the term paper she had to work on, because when the train pulled into Eastfield station, she went her way, and I went mine.

Cara and Billy were just leaving the house as I arrived. I was debating whether to tell Cara the news, when a car slowed down and parked right in front of us. I saw a pair of legs in faded jeans first, then the long, thin body that went with the jeans, wearing a khaki-colored sweater that I'd seen in my father's L. L. Bean catalogue.

"Sam," said Billy, and I felt myself flick at my hair like Margot does when she sees a guy, only Sam caught me doing it and said, "Your hair looks fine."

I couldn't believe it. "What are you, a hairdresser or something?" I said to him.

"I'm a friend of Billy's," said Sam, laughing.

"So you're a jock." I was merciless. I was beating back shock therapy, and Sam was in the way.

Except he liked it. His green eyes widened, and he held up his hands and said, "Not guilty, not guilty!"

"She has a thing against jocks," said Billy apologetically.

"Don't tell me what I have." I could see Cara pacing, and

it was her turn. "So how come Dad is going into the hospital and nobody told me?"

Cara looked blankly at me. "Nobody told me, either. What's the deal?"

Billy flung an arm around Sam, and they went off by a bush.

"Electric shock treatment," I said, so loudly that the boys looked over.

"Not in front of a stranger," whispered Cara.

eighteen

On Monday morning, I searched the halls for a sign of Alex and found Sam instead. I turned to go the other way, but he did an about-face, radar blinking, and called after me.

"How's your dad?" he said when he caught up with me.

"Okay," I said coldly. None of your business.

"It's going to be fine," he said, walking beside me with such long strides that it took two of mine to keep up with one of his.

"My uncle is a psychiatrist," Sam explained. "He said that shock treatment is much more sophisticated now."

"Great," I said, laying on the sarcasm. "I'm so glad the whole world knows about my father."

Sam ignored me. "He said it's called electroconvulsive therapy—ECT, for short. It sometimes helps in cases that don't respond to drugs or medication."

"ECT? Very cute. I particularly like the convulsive part." By this time, I was so mad I was practically jogging. "Are you sure you're not Billy's cousin or something?" I panted. I reached my locker and fiddled for my combination.

"Why?" said Sam, leaning against the lockers and looking intently at me with those green eyes of his.

"He reads to us practically every day from his jock psychology manual," I said.

Sam rubbed his temple with an index finger. "Why do you hate him so much?" he said. "He's crazy about Cara, and he thinks you're pretty nice too."

I yanked open my locker door so that it slammed hard against the metal. "I don't hate him," I said, knowing I had on my bulldog face. And how come only pretty nice?

"It sure sounds like you do," said Sam, glancing at his watch and murmuring, "Calculus!"

He put his hand on my shoulder as he walked by. "Just try not to worry about your father."

"I'm not," I said, and I yelled to his back, "And I don't hate him!"

So that was that. I was screaming down hallways, and everybody was watching me, and Alex chose that moment to arrive on the scene.

"What's going on?" he said, looking at me curiously. "Who was that?"

"A friend of my sister's," I told him.

"So tell him to go bother your sister." Alex took my hand and pulled me toward him.

We walked down the hallway, holding hands, with my cheeks burning because it felt like the whole world was watching, and this wasn't holding hands in the playground, no ring-around-a-rosy, this was in the high school hallway, a mini-declaration, passing Jimmy and Lynn Baker, and Margot and Angie, who raised her eyebrows just a little but smiled like she was really happy for me.

Alex came over that night and met my parents. It reminded me of one of those half-hour family television programs, where the parents quiz the boyfriend, only it was just my mother asking the questions, while my father stood next to her like a bodyguard.

We went to my room to study, and I was half hoping that my mother would tell me to keep the door open. She didn't, so I shut it.

"Your dad doesn't say much, does he?" Alex lounged on my bed, and I resisted telling him to take off his shoes, because I didn't want him getting ideas about taking anything else off.

"He's like that," I said vaguely.

"Your mother is the ball-breaker, huh?" He had his arms folded behind his head, and his rippling muscles didn't do much for me then. In fact, I felt like hitting him.

"Not really," I said, my mother's defender in an instant. "He's been . . . out of it for a while, and she has to do everything." I sat at my desk and pulled out my history notebook, flipping through the pages like I was looking for something, hoping he wouldn't ask me any questions.

Alex patted the bed, and I perched at the edge. One slip, and I'd fall flat on my butt.

"What's the notebook for?" he said, smiling.

"I *do* need to study," I said, riffling through the pages again.

Alex took the book out of my hands and tossed it on the floor. "You have other things to learn," he said, pulling my head toward him the way Richie had, so that I froze, and my heart began beating furiously, and I became an ice maiden, and he was pulling and I was resisting until he got the message and stopped.

"What's the story?" he said quietly. "You were hot the other night."

Hot? I hated the word, and in a flash, I hated Alex.

"I thought we had a good time," he said, and his eyes had

this hurt look in them that reminded me of my father. I touched his cheek, and suddenly we were kissing again.

My mother surprised us with a knock, and we were back in that television sitcom, because she walked in with a bag of potato chips and two cans of lemon-lime seltzer, and we sprang apart like two ingenues who didn't know how to act. I've got to hand it to my mom. She must have figured that we couldn't do two things at the same time, and she was right, because the evening changed, and we ate potato chips and drank soda and talked a little. I should have known that studying in a bedroom was about as likely as watching the movie in a drive-in.

Sam called the next night, and suddenly I was the belle of the ball and two guys wanted to fill my dance card. I had to let Sam down gently, only I wasn't sure how a New Jersey belle would do it, so I blew it.

"I'm seeing someone," I said, and it sounded like I was forty years old.

"Oh," said Sam, and there was a silence. "So when does your dad go in?"

"Why do you want to know?" I said. "Why are you so interested in my father?"

"Because Billy wants to visit with Cara, and I said I'd drive him. His car is in the shop."

"Billy?" I was amazed. "Why would Billy want to visit him?"

"He *is* your sister's boyfriend," said Sam. "They're like an old married couple by now. He likes your father."

"How could he like him? He's never known him when he was normal," I blurted out.

"He still wants to visit," said Sam.

"He's going in this weekend," I said gruffly.

I hung up and went to Cara's bedroom to see her, half of the old married couple.

"How come the whole world has to visit Dad?" I said to her.

Cara put down the college catalogue she was reading. "Only Billy," she said.

"How come Sam has to butt in and drive you?"

"We wouldn't all fit in Mom's car, and Mom said it was all right." She held up the catalogue. "Which do you think? Temple University or Syracuse with Billy? I have to make up my mind."

"Syracuse," I said vehemently. "It's further away."

"Billy says you're the moodiest person he's ever met," Cara shouted after me as I walked out the door.

"And his friend is the dopiest," I shot back.

It's truly wonderful having a sister to confide in. Such a comfort.

We visited my father a week after he'd entered the hospital. Rachel and I sat in the back of the car, caretakers of the food we were bringing. Rachel held the cake, in its white bakery box, upright in her lap.

"Black Forest cake is his favorite." Rachel sounded excited, like we were going to Disneyland or something.

"Do you think he'll be any better?" I spoke to the back of my mother's head.

"The doctor said that the results can be quite dramatic," said my mother.

"What's he going to do, start reciting *Hamlet*?" I felt nasty saying it. Nobody answered me anyway. Would my father know, by looking into my eyes, that the week home without him had been a relief? I clasped my hands together, and they were cold and clammy, even though a shaft of sunlight fell across them. My mother continued her teeth-grinding driving, with my grandmother sitting next to her, yammering about the price of coffee. Grandma didn't seem to notice that my mother grunted and braked every other minute. She just jammed one hand against the dashboard whenever my mother began punching her foot on the pedal like a maniac. Of course, maniac isn't a word I should use so loosely, since I was thinking about electroconvulsive therapy, and Sam had made a further point of telling me that his uncle said they usually gave it to patients who were catatonic. So how come my father, who was still vacuuming and grocery shopping, was getting it? Instead of straitjackets and barred windows, now I was conjuring up convulsions—lots of foam and jerking around—while Grandma still jabbered about prices and Rachel talked about chocolate cake again, and my mother grunted and braked in the front seat, to the strains of a Strauss waltz. I was beginning to wonder who was the crazy one.

It was my mother's idea to have a picnic, because there was a riverside park near the hospital, and my father was getting a day pass. When we entered the building, I saw my mother hesitate, just for a split second. She had a weird look on her face—kind of like terror. She turned to me and asked if I would go with her to get my father, while Rachel stayed with my grandmother.

We went over to the reception desk, and while my mother asked questions, I looked around for bars, but I didn't see any. Then a guard pressed a buzzer, and somebody buzzed back and clicked us through a heavy door. That was the only sign of anybody being locked up.

We entered a large room with a few tables, two ugly brown couches, and a handful of people sitting around. I recognized my father by his red hunting cap—he always embarrassed my mother by wearing it to weddings and such, then taking it off at the last moment as he walked into the reception hall.

His face broke into a huge smile when he saw us, and he pushed himself away from the table and stood.

"Hurray!" he shouted as he walked toward us. He hugged my mother first, and then me, hard, and I didn't smell any sizzling electricity on him. I expected him to feel weak, to stumble or something, but his arms gripped me like the wrestler he used to be in college.

"Get me out of here," he said, in a stage whisper. My mother looked alarmed at first, until she saw his face. He was grinning from ear to ear. Then he peered right and he peered left, gripping our arms as he scouted the hallway. "The guards are having dinner," he said in a low voice. "We can make our escape now!"

My mother said, "Ben!" in an exasperated tone that reminded me of the old days, and then she said, "Please take off that silly hat! You look like you're about to go deerstalking!"

My father laughed, and it startled me, because I couldn't remember the last time I'd heard it.

He put his head back and closed his eyes as we left the building and hit the spring air.

"Are you dizzy, Ben?" said my grandmother, concern in her voice.

"I'm happy," said my father. "Happy to leave that place."

"Is it awful?" said Rachel, taking my father's hand.

"The treatment is no worse than the dentist," said my father. "The inmates are a little weird."

We took our picnic lunch out of the car and walked toward the river. Cara and Billy had arrived, and I could see Sam in the distance, watching some old men play chess.

Cara hugged my father, and Billy gave him a handshake.

"Hi, Billy," said my father. "Good of you to come. How did all of you fit in the car?"

"Sam took us," said Cara, pointing vaguely toward the chessplayers.

"Invite him over for a picnic lunch," said my father, and he turned and kissed my mother on the forehead.

All of us sat around the picnic table, eating tuna-fish sandwiches, and pickles, and potato salad, and Grandma's coleslaw. Then my mother took out a huge thermos and poured steaming cups of coffee for my father and grandmother.

"I'll have one," I said. It looked so tempting, with the steam curling up into the air, and my mother poured a cup for me without saying a word. Then my grandmother said, "It'll make you nervous."

"I'm nervous already," I said. My father smiled and said, "I'm a little nervous myself," and then my mother started to laugh, and my father started to laugh, and Grandma and Cara and Rachel and I started laughing too, and I really felt we were a family.

"So what's the food like?" said Sam when we'd stopped, and that started us laughing all over again.

After lunch, Cara convinced me to ride back with them. Sam and Billy had done their macho bit in the park playground, on the monkey bars alongside the kids, while Cara and I watched in a kind of sisterly silence. My father seemed better, and the playground looked busy and jolly with children, and Sam looked almost handsome with his forearms straining and his hair glinting in the spring sun.

As we walked back to the car, even the homeless men sprawled against the playground fence looked less threatening to me. When Sam stopped and spoke to one of them, I stood quietly by and didn't draw back.

"I always think one of them is going to be my uncle," he told me as we started walking again.

"Did your uncle lose his job or something?"

Sam shook his head. "He made it back from Vietnam, but he never made it back . . . in the head."

"That's awful," I said.

"My aunt doesn't know where he went. He just stopped living at home one day, and a friend of theirs saw him on the street." Sam waved his hand at a makeshift cardboard house. "Living in one of those."

"So she can't remarry."

Sam shrugged. "She told me she waited so long for him to come home. Now she's still waiting. She dreams about it, that someday he'll come walking through the door and give her a big hug, and then he'll kiss their little boy, Jason, and swing him up in the air. Only Jason is practically my height now."

We reached the car, and Sam unlocked my door first. It felt weird to be treated like I was the important one, when Cara was the one the boys always paid attention to. Sitting in the front seat, feeling like a big shot, with my sister in the back, I kept checking out Sam's profile when he wasn't looking.

"When we got inside the hospital," I turned to tell Cara, "Dad pretended he was escaping. You know, the way he used to when he'd fool around. He had Mom going for a minute there."

"Well, come on," said Sam. "You'd have to be crazy to want to stay in a place like that."

I gave him a sharp look, and he pounded the side of his head, and that started me laughing hysterically.

"You look pretty that way," Sam told me.

"Whoaaa," said Billy from the back seat, and I could hear Cara hit him, but I didn't turn around because I was too busy wondering if I looked as pretty with my cat-that-ate-the-canary smile spread across my face.

nineteen

Mr. Shapiro named the poem about my father "Black Snowman" and planned on making it the first piece in the *Pen and Quill*.

"That is, if you have no objection," he said, widening his eyes.

"Why should I object?" I said to him.

"Considering your father . . . ," said Mr. Shapiro, winking at me like we had some kind of conspiracy.

Carl, the editor, showed me a weird-looking drawing of a black snowman lying in bed. It made me want to puke, but I told him it was great. Who was I to complain?

Mr. Shapiro took me aside and asked how my father was doing.

"Better," I told him, checking my watch to see if I'd be late meeting Alex outside.

"You see?" said Mr. Shapiro, beaming. "I told you things would work out."

"How's your wife doing?" I said.

"In the pink," said Mr. Shapiro.

I glanced at my watch again. It was early yet, and Mr.

Shapiro bobbed his bald head at me. He had that puppy-dog look in his eye, a look you could trust, and taking a deep breath, I said, "Did she ever have any electric shock treatment?"

Mr. Shapiro switched to his concerned look and shook his head. "Never," he said. "But they were considering it at one point."

"My father had it. He's coming home from the hospital this weekend."

The minute I said it, I was sorry. Mr. Shapiro was nodding his head, and the concerned look was getting deeper and I felt I had to make it worth his while or something—like telling him that my father died the minute they attached the electrodes.

He was shaking his head now. "He must have been in bad shape," he said. "How's your mother coping?"

She was electrocuted holding his hand, dodo. "She's doing pretty well," I said. "My grandmother says we come from strong stock. Rock stock, she calls it."

Mr. Shapiro smiled, but I could tell he was relieved. "And have you seen your father?" he said. "How's he doing?"

"My father said it wasn't much worse than the dentist," I told him. But Mr. Shapiro wasn't looking at me anymore. He was blank-eyed and staring past me.

"What can I do for you, Alex?" I heard him say.

My heart lurched. I'd never bothered telling Alex. I figured what he didn't know wouldn't hurt him.

Alex nodded his head toward me. "I'm waiting for Zoe."

I gathered up my things and gave my own version of a wink to Mr. Shapiro, only it was more like a nervous tic, because Alex sounded angry, and he had this weird look in his eyes, and it scared me to death.

"What the hell was all that about?" he said.

"My father," I said quickly. "He was having some problems, so they put him in the hospital."

"What kind of hospital?" Alex snarled. "Don't you mean a loony bin?"

"I mean a hospital!" I said defensively. "The doctors say he's responding nicely." I rattled off what my mother had told us.

Alex let out a whistle. "I thought something wasn't kosher."

"How would you know?" I snapped. "You thought Yom Kippur was a smoked fish."

"Don't get testy," said Alex. "I only meant I thought there was something a little . . . off about your father."

"It's a sickness," I told him. "Would you think there was something a little off about . . ." I was sputtering now, searching for the right disease. ". . . heart disease?" I said at last.

Alex shook his head, like he was trying to get water out of his ear. "It gives me the creeps."

"He'll be home this weekend," I said stiffly. "And speaking of creeps . . ." I turned my back on him and started walking away.

"Hey." Alex grabbed hold of my hand and pulled me to him, caveman style. "Come on, Zoe. All that mental stuff makes me kind of nervous, that's all."

I pulled loose. "If it makes you so nervous, maybe you shouldn't come around anymore." My heart started thumping again.

"You don't mean that."

I shrugged and looked down at the floor. Talk me out of it, talk me out of it, I chanted to myself.

The silence was deafening.

Then I heard him say, "Maybe it's for the best."

And when I looked up, he was gone.

Angie met me at the library after supper and tried to cheer me up.

"You didn't really like him as much in real life as you did when you had a crush on him." Angie put her face directly in front of mine. "Come on," she said, "admit it."

I wasn't buying it. "I told him not to come around anymore, and he jumped at the chance."

"You had nothing in common, Zoe. You said so yourself."

"I didn't mean it." The librarian was looking our way, and I opened a book. "He was a great kisser," I whispered.

"You said he wanted to go all the way!" Angie hissed at me. "That he was going too fast!"

"He was great-looking." I let out a long sigh. I sniffed and let out another sigh. Holding my hand in front of my mouth, I breathed and sniffed again. My breath smelled awful. "No wonder he dumped me," I whispered. "Do you have any mints?"

Angie fished in her pocket and pulled out a moldy green disk. "Here," she said, handing it to me. "My last. And he didn't dump you."

I made a face. "Are you sure this is a mint?"

"It's an upper," Angie growled at me. "You are driving me crazy. Eat it and shut up."

I popped it into my mouth and tried to settle down to some real work, but Hurricane Margot was rushing through the library doors like she was ready to blow us over.

She cut right to the chase. "Is it true you broke up with

Alex?" she said, holding her face so close to mine that I was glad for the mint.

"Sort of," I said. "But I never—"

"She never figured he would be such a jerk," interrupted Angie.

"Well, I heard it straight from Alex, and I figured you wouldn't mind." Margot flipped her hair out and fished in her coat pocket, extracting a lipstick.

"You figured I wouldn't mind what?" A feeling of doom was descending on me. I waited while Margot applied her lip gloss.

"Alex wants us to get it together."

"Get it together?" I was a ventriloquist's dummy, mouth open, words coming from somewhere else.

"You know. He says he's always had the hots for me." Margot widened her eyes. "You don't care, do you? I mean, you were the one that broke up."

"I couldn't care less," I heard the dummy say. I didn't look at Angie.

"What about your playwriter?" said Angie, my friend, while I tried to recover.

"Oh, him." Margot dismissed him with a wave of her hand. "Not my type."

"Too wild?" said Angie.

"Wild?" Margot looked puzzled. "He wasn't wild. He was too . . . intellectual. You know. He wanted to talk about his friend's play afterward."

"Too much talk, huh?" Angie kept up the conversation, while I willed myself to look nonchalant, like losing Alex was part of my life plan.

I cleared my throat. "What about Jimmy?" I croaked.

"Jimmy's going out with Linda Eckert." Margot put her

face in front of mine again. "So what's Alex like?" she said. "Wet or dry?"

Angie saved me again. "Aren't you afraid they'll compare notes?"

Margot laughed. "So? Nobody's ever complained!"

I tried to recall Angie's theory, something about Margot and her father, something about approval, but it didn't help. I was a failure. I'd lost Alex for good, and I hadn't even had him long enough to know if I missed him.

Margot was preening herself as I gathered up my books and said goodbye. If I didn't leave, Margot would catch me with tears in my eyes.

Angie followed faithfully. "She'd go with Grumpy John if she had a free night," she whispered in my ear as we pushed through the library doors.

"So?" I walked with my eyes glued to the sidewalk.

"So as long as it walks and talks and has a zipper—"

"Alex is *not* Grumpy John."

"There are plenty of fish—"

"If you finish that sentence I'm going to kill myself," I told her, quickening the pace. "You sound just like my mother!"

"Your mother is right," said Angie, panting. "What are we doing here, race-walking?"

"I could use the exercise. I'm a fat pig." I heard myself whining. I was like a record with a scratch on it, repeating myself over and over again—I'm stupid, I'm fat, I deserve it, I'm stupid, I'm fat, I deserve it—only Angie wouldn't listen. She took off the scratched record and put on another one.

"You're beautiful and talented," she started.

"I don't want to hear it," I said, holding my hands to my ears.

"There are lots of nice guys out there," Angie continued, prying a hand off my ear.

"Like who?" I said to her.

"Like that Sam guy you told me about. Remember how great you said he looked, riding on the seesaw or something?"

"Hanging from the monkey bars," I said. A little light went on in my head, and I remembered how good it felt sitting next to him in the front seat of the car.

"Hanging from the monkey bars, then. You liked him, I could tell."

Slowing the pace, I remembered how he said I looked pretty when I laughed. I couldn't remember laughing with Alex. I allowed myself just a small smile.

"That's better," said Angie.

The smile was gone by Saturday morning.

I lay in bed considering my track record. Saved by a pair of elasticized panty hose from John. I was *so* uncool. Grossed out by college boy Richie. He was a creep, and I was a total washout. Told Alex not to come around anymore. And he didn't. Dumbo! He probably really hated the way I kissed, thought I was a total prude. Threw away the one chance I had with Sam. Why would he want me now? I'd told him I was involved. And if he did? I would probably be an uncool total washout. Or he would.

I wanted to stay in bed forever, but it reminded me too much of my father and the Big D. He was coming home today. So how come I felt like somebody had died? I jumped out of bed, lay down on the carpet, and did some sit-ups. Anything to keep myself from thinking the worst thought in the world: Maybe I was depressed.

I was glad to find Rachel in the kitchen. I made myself some tea and sat down next to her. Rachel offered me a bagel, but I shook my head. I didn't feel like eating. The blackness was descending.

Rachel didn't notice. "You should drink more milk," she said. "We have a lot of hunchbacks in our family."

I sipped my tea and ignored her.

"Ruth eats Tums. They have a lot of calcium in them."

"I'm thrilled for her," I said. Ruth was Rachel's therapist, and we were treated to a daily dose of her golden words.

"Are you angry about something? Ruth says you shouldn't keep your anger in."

"Ruth is a pill." I eyed my sister. It was true she was looking a lot better. She'd lost some weight. She looked happier.

Rachel got all huffy and said, "Ruth says I need validation."

"I'll validate you to the moon!" I shouted, but Rachel was giving me her Bambi look now, and I didn't want to feel like a monster *and* a failure. "Sorry," I said.

"It's okay. I know you feel bad about Alex." Rachel brightened. "Hey, I think *Lassie* is on now. Do you want to watch it with me?"

I made a face but followed Rachel into the living room. What the heck, I could use a good cry, and by the time Lassie had saved some dopey little boy from being bitten by a rattlesnake that got into his house in a box of fruit or something, I was bawling buckets.

Rachel handed me a tissue. "Your nose is running," she said.

I took the tissue and wiped my eyes. "That felt good," I said.

Rachel blew her nose. "Ruth says that crying is a good outlet. Oops!" She covered her mouth with her hand. "Sorry."

I had to laugh. "You like her a lot, don't you," I said.

"She makes me feel like . . ." Rachel looked shyly at me. "Promise you won't laugh."

I promised.

"She makes me feel like I'm not crazy."

"I could use some of that," I said.

"Oh, I talked to her about you," Rachel said quickly.

"What did you say?" I was glad. Maybe Ruth had the answer. Maybe Ruth could tell me why I had so much trouble with boyfriends. Maybe Ruth knew all about feeling so angry that you thought you were going to burst.

"I told her about your boyfriend and how he broke up with you because he thought Dad was nuts."

"He didn't exactly think Dad was nuts. He just wasn't . . . comfortable with it." I switched channels on the TV, caught snatches of Huckleberry Hound, New Kids on the Block, a bunch of happy dinosaurs playing together.

Rachel was warming up. "If you really want to know, Ruth says that lots of people are afraid of mental illness. It's like cancer. They're afraid they're going to catch it."

I settled on the new *Gidget*, but after a minute or so, I couldn't stand it anymore. A world of happy endings. I punched the Off button so hard that Rachel jumped.

"It's all a crock," I said. "He probably broke up with me because I . . . I didn't know how to kiss. Or I bored him. Something like that." I could feel the tears welling up in my eyes, and I brushed them away.

"Kiss?" Rachel said the word like it was some kind of dead animal. Then she shuddered, so I changed the subject.

My mom made a big deal about my father's homecoming. She treated him like a war hero, cooking his favorite meal, setting the table with the best dishes, putting his slippers by his favorite easy chair. She even played country and western music on the radio. True love. I was surprised she hadn't put up streamers.

I was glad to see him, I really was. But when he went to kiss me hello, I turned my cheek away. I was the ice maiden again, only this time it was my father, not John or Richie or Alex, and anyway, it had nothing to do with sex.

During supper, my father ate the eggplant casserole with such relish that it made me feel sick. My mother hovered over him. Every time Cara went into the kitchen for something, she put her arms around him from behind. Rachel chattered incessantly about Ruth and school. My father sat there, smiling and soaking it all up. I sat there in silence, the sick one, the one who couldn't forgive him. My father didn't seem to notice.

After supper I went to my room. I lay face down on my bed. When the telephone rang, I didn't jump up, and when there was a knock on the door, I said, "I'm busy."

My father poked his head inside.

"I'm tired," I told him, peering at him through my hair.

"I'll only be a minute," he said as he walked inside.

I rolled over onto my back and propped my hands under my head. I could see that he was holding something.

He came closer. In his hand was the new *Pen and Quill* I'd just brought home. My heart did a flip-flop.

"I just wanted to tell you," he said. "The poem. It's very good."

My throat felt dry. "Thank you," I whispered.

My father sat on the side of the bed. There were tears in his eyes.

"I'm so sorry," he said, and he kissed me on the forehead. This time I didn't turn away.

That night, I fell into a deep sleep. I can't remember when I slept better. I had made my father cry. I should have felt terrible about that, but I didn't. I felt washed clean, even though I hadn't taken a shower. The next morning, I sat down for breakfast, the boyfriendless *enfant terrible* who had reduced her father to tears, and I buttered myself a bagel and ate it. So much for my depression.

My father was still kind of quiet, but his eyes were different. They were alive. When Rachel started in on a second bagel, he didn't tell her she'd get fat. He said, "I hope you're going out for a walk with me today, kiddo."

When the telephone rang and Cara jumped up and said, "It's Billy, for me," my father gave my mother a look. "What are they, joined at the hip?" he said, loud enough for Cara to hear.

"Daaaaaad," she said. Such a familiar whine, but one I hadn't heard in a long time.

He washed the breakfast dishes without being asked. My mother dried. There was a wariness about her, kind of like a little kid with a balloon. She loved the balloon but was afraid it would pop.

After cleanup, my father went to his study. We could hear the sound of typing. My mother put her feet up on the couch and read the Sunday newspaper for a while. Then she made fresh coffee and took a cup to my father. I could hear them talking through the walls.

Angie came over at lunchtime and marveled at the change in me.

"What happened?" she said.

"Nothing," I told her. "I've acquired a new maturity overnight."

Angie laughed. "I've heard that one before."

"I don't need a man to validate me." Ruth and Rachel would have been proud.

Angie was downright skeptical. "Thank you, Mrs. Freud," she said.

"I have my writing, I have my friends and family," I said. "I don't need any more than that."

"What happened to Sam's sinewy arms on the monkey bars?"

"Part of the past," I said. "The same goes for Alex's biceps."

After Angie left, I went up to my room and found an envelope, slipped under my door. "Zoe dear" was scrawled across the front, in my father's chicken-scratch handwriting. Inside it, typewritten, was a poem.

> The zombie, the goof-off, the dummy, the fretter,
> Your father, ex-robot, is really much better.
> So put on your best clothes, your favorite sweater,
> Your father, ex-zombie, is better, much better.
> He's punchy, quite munchy, a rake, a go-getter.
> Your father, the valiant, the brave one, is better.

Across the bottom of the page, my father had written, "Anyone for ice cream?"

I could see my mother wanted to go with us, but my father shook his head. He placed his red hunting cap strategically on top of his bald spot and cocked it rakishly. I guess he thought he looked good, instead of goofy, but I wasn't afraid of the goofiness. As long as he didn't look *crazy*.

"You're wearing that?" said my mother, but her words faded into a smile.

My father took my arm, and we began to stroll. That's always been all you can do with my father. Walk slowly, drive slowly, talk slowly—a liquid kind of living until the depression, when sludge took over.

"How about an Italian ice?" he said.

"Fine," I told him, and we headed toward Grumpy John's because they had twenty-some-odd flavors and I was running through them in my head: cherry, rainbow, lemon, lime, piña colada, chocolate, rum raisin. The aroma of pizza hit us as we walked through the door, and I continued reciting my mantra: tangerine, peach, vanilla, orange, Lynn Baker and Sam, and Angie was right and I was wrong, because it mattered very much to me that they were sitting together, head to head, knee to knee, at a table in the corner of Grumpy John's.

My face must have changed, or maybe my father noticed that I was hiding behind him like he was a shield, because he said quietly, "Are you okay?" and then his eyes, his alive eyes, noticed Sam.

He took off his hat and tucked it in his pocket. At that moment, Sam looked up, and I turned my head away. I heard my father say, "Hi, Sam, good to see you," real soft, real casual, and Sam stood up and came over.

"How are you, Mr. Cohen?" he said, but it felt like his eyes were boring into my head.

"I'm doing good," said my father, and then he said to Grumpy John's daughter, "A piña colada ice, please," which floored me, because he knew just what he wanted.

"How's it going, Zoe?" I looked up, and Sam was staring at me. His green eyes were as nice as ever.

"Hunky-dory," I answered, unoriginal, dopey. I could have killed myself.

Grumpy John's daughter was also staring at me, and off the top of my head I said, "Cherry," only my least favorite flavor, but anything to look away, and I took the white cup she handed me and licked it and licked it until Sam said goodbye and wandered back to his seat.

173

We walked outside, and my father took out his hunting cap and put it back on his head and I continued licking my cherry ice until my tongue and my lips were cherry-colored.

twenty

My father and I walked home in silence. When we reached the house, I loitered. I plucked at bushes, kicked stones, anything to avoid the emptiness of my bedroom. My father kept me company. He finished his Italian ice, pulled idly at the pleated edges of the cup. Then he threw it into the garbage can.

"The garden needs work," he said, digging with his fingers into the ground and removing some offending green. I watched him bend and dig. If I squinted, I could picture him old. I could picture him ancient, dead and buried, and me, his daughter, never really knowing him. He sat down on the steps and picked up the local advertising circular that was lying there.

"Dollar ninety-nine for a half gallon of Breyer's ice cream. That's good, isn't it?" he asked me.

"I guess so," I said, "but I'm too fat to eat it." I addressed the air. "Why would he want *her?*"

My father surprised me by actually knowing what I was talking about. "She's approachable," he said.

"You mean she's easy."

"I wouldn't know. She just looked like someone who wouldn't scare the boys away." My father turned a page.

"And I would?"

"You may not *feel* self-assured, Zoe, but you carry yourself as if you are." He held up the circular. "How about you kids getting me a leaf-blower for my birthday?"

I felt a slow burn starting. He was changing the subject already. He was gone, unavailable. Thanks for nothing.

But he surprised me again. "He certainly seemed interested when we had the picnic," he said.

"He did?" I watched my father crumple the circular into a ball.

"He couldn't take his eyes off you."

"He couldn't?" My eyes filled with tears. "So how come I screwed up and picked the wrong guy?"

His smile was gentle. "We live and learn, honey."

"I don't think I'll ever learn."

"Never say never, Zoe." My father stood up and dusted off his pants. "I never thought I'd get better." His voice was so low that I could barely hear him.

"But you're better?"

"I hope so."

I wanted him to say yes, emphatically, without a single reservation, and he must have seen it in my eyes. "I'm not going to promise you I'll never get depressed again, Zoe."

"I'm not asking you to," I said, but I was lying.

He held out his arms. We hugged so hard that we grunted from the effort.

"I'll try not to disappear," he said.

I didn't ask him what he meant.

When I pulled away, I said to him, "About that leaf-blower."

"Yes?" My father looked as eager as a little kid.

"Would a rake do?"

He threw the ball of paper at me, and we walked into the house, laughing.

The next day was Monday.

I hate Monday, because it's Monday and because I have gym that day. At school, I avoided everybody. I was a horse with blinders. I didn't look left and I didn't look right. I examined every inch of the rubberized floor in the halls. Angie was the only face I recognized. She led me from class to class, so that I didn't have to look at anyone by the name of Alex or Margot or Lynn or Sam.

We played field hockey in gym. I like the out-of-doors, really. It's running around in it with a stick in my hand that I'm not too crazy about. Mrs. Konig separated us into two teams. She has a good heart, she truly does, because she chooses the teams. That way, no one feels bad because she's the last one picked. But today, Mrs. Konig was a little out of it. It seemed she put all of the nerds and clods, which includes me and Angie, on the same side. Shana Sinclair, who wears such thick spectacles that her eyes look like they're under a magnifying glass, was the first one chosen. She's even klutzier than me or Melanie or Ava, and we're pretty bad.

Anyway, the klutzolas took their places on the field. Each of us was guarded by a racehorse. Jimmy's new filly, Linda Eckert, was running rings around me, but I didn't care. My heart just wasn't in the game. All the young racehorses were chomping at the bit—Lynn and Margot, Alexa, Janie—ready to cream us. They were the ones who were tan all year long and walked around the locker room stark naked, without looking the least bit embarrassed. They *liked* their little sticks. They *liked* field hockey. They *liked* their bodies.

I was standing there admiring the scenery when I saw a racehorse named Allison hit the puck so hard that it came

Angie's way, and Angie and I were supposed to score, so she passed the puck to me and I went running, scooping it along as I went, until I looked up and there was Lynn Baker, stick slashing away at my puck, and I wouldn't let her have it—no, I wouldn't—and my elbow went out and found some soft flesh and I heard a screech and I raced past the klutzolas Shana and Melanie, with their mouths hanging open, and there was Margot, a shit grin on her face as she guarded her goalposts, and she wasn't keeping me from scoring because I was a powerhouse, I was a locomotive, and I steamrolled that puck past her and leaped into the air like I was a Dallas Cowboys cheerleader, to the sounds of clapping.

It was without doubt the greatest single athletic moment of my life.

In the locker room, Angie and I strutted, puffed up, with our towels knotted around our Jockey For Her underwear, like we were doing an aftershave commercial. Lynn Baker was naked, with her towel draped around her neck, but she had a slight hobble, and she was holding her side. Margot was pouting.

Angie and I got dressed, side by side. She couldn't look at me. She just pressed her lips together hard, and every once in a while I heard a strange noise bubble out. We burst through the gymnasium doors and into the hallway, a pair of laughing hyenas. Somehow, I was able to look at everybody.

"Zoe!" A male voice called my name, and I turned around quickly, a racehorse, so my hair swung, but it was only Mr. Shapiro.

"Could I see you for a moment?" I followed him into his classroom, and he motioned for me to sit down. "How's everything going at home?" he said to me.

"Fine." A bunch of *Pen and Quills* were sitting on his desk, and for a split second I remembered the tears in my father's eyes.

"I want to thank you for doing such a great job on the magazine," Mr. Shapiro continued, tapping the pile with his index finger. "It's excellent." He reached down and opened up a desk drawer. "We had some late submissions that I thought you might like to see."

No, thank you, I felt like saying, you can throw them in the garbage, but I took the folder from him and stuck it between my books. I stood up. "Thanks, Mr. Shapiro," I said. "For everything." I felt kind of tender toward his bald head, now that I was a racehorse with a father who cared, now that the school year was almost over and next year I wouldn't have to be in cahoots with Mr. Shapiro, because next year, I hoped, the word "depression" could only be applied to the economy and not to the Cohen family, ever ever ever.

"Don't forget to check out those poems," he said. "Particularly the one on top."

"I won't," I said to him.

I remembered the folder that night, when I flopped across my bed and my books slid to the floor. Three sheets of paper scattered across the room, and I picked them up reluctantly.

I was tempted not to read them at all, but the responsible little voice that my parents must have cultivated in me for years stopped me from chucking them away. The first piece was a "Roses are red" disaster. I threw it in the wastebasket. The second one was by Linda Eckert. She liked kitties. The kitties joined the roses in the garbage. I held the third one over the basket and glanced at it. I sat down on the bed and read:

He sees her bouncing by him, she doesn't have a care.
He speaks, she doesn't answer, he's attracted to her hair.
He touches her, she stops . . . she giggles and she talks.
He looks at her, a beauty, but she screeches, belches, squawks.
He's chosen her, it's doomsday, toys-in-the-attic time.
He was looking for a gold mine. Instead? He found a dime.
They played, they ran, they drifted, with her mouth shut they
     had fun.
If he'd only caught the other . . . Then? He would have had
     the sun.

The name at the bottom of the page was "Sam Prelutsky."

Mr. Shapiro was always on our backs about interpreting poetry. I never worked harder interpreting this one. And the only conclusion I came to, every time, was that if I was "the other," he liked *me* better than he did Lynn Baker. Period.

I held the piece of paper signed with Sam Prelutsky's name up to the light, like I was looking for a flaw in a precious gem. I didn't call Angie. I wanted to keep my diamond a secret, just a while longer . . . except that I felt like calling Sam.

The telephone book was in the front closet downstairs. I crept into the hallway detective-style, hiding in the shadows and avoiding the creaky parts of the wooden floor. Music was coming from Rachel's room, and I didn't even mind it. That was weird. She was growing up. Cara was out somewhere with Billy. I started down the stairs and stopped midway. My parents were talking in the kitchen, probably over coffee. Soft talk, without the high pitch of my mother's voice, which I had become used to hearing. I continued downstairs and began to slide the closet door open. It stuck. I pushed hard on it, but it wouldn't budge. I rattled it. Gave it a kick.

"Watch the paint job," my father said in my ear. I hadn't heard him coming. He took hold of the door and wrenched it back on the track. "What do you need?" he said.

"The telephone book," I told him. I could feel a blush start at my neck and rise up.

"Who are you looking for?" said my father. "At the risk of being nosy."

"Sam," I said. "I'm looking for Sam."

"Good," said my father. "He seems like a nice fellow." He reached into the closet, pulled out the telephone book, and handed it to me. "I'm all for it."

"You're all for what?" I said, clutching the book to me.

"For asking a man out, if you really like him. Why should the man have to risk rejection every time?" He winked at me and turned to walk toward the kitchen.

"I just want to talk to him," I called after my father.

"Talk?" said my father. "Talk is good."

Talk is good. Call Sam. He seems like a nice fellow. Who *was* this new father, shooting off his mouth all the time, giving his opinion? I'd have to get used to it.

Upstairs, I closed the door to my parents' bedroom and sat down on the bed. The telephone stood there on the nightstand, beckoning. I took a pencil from the drawer and found the *P*'s in the phone book. There were only two Prelutskys, and I wrote down the one that said Arthur. Helen was the other. I wondered if she was the wife of the uncle who lived in the streets.

I picked up the receiver and put it down again. My heart raced, and I hadn't even started dialing. We still had the kind of telephone you dialed. My father didn't like pushing buttons—joked that if he wanted to play the piano, he'd buy one.

I dialed the number with a shaking index finger. A woman picked up the phone with a tuneful "Hellooooo!"

"Is Sam there?" I said. My voice sounded like I'd just gotten out of bed. I cleared my throat as she called out "Sammy!"

Sammy. She must have called him that when he was a baby. Sammy.

"Hello?" His voice sounded gruff. He didn't sing out like his mother did.

"Sammy?" I heard myself say.

"Who is this?" said Sammy, unamused.

"It's Zoe."

"Zoe?"

"Zoe Cohen," I said.

He was silent for a moment, and then he said, "There's only one Zoe."

"Well," I said. "This is she."

Sam started laughing, and so did I, and he never asked me what I was calling about. He just told me he was taking me to the beach on Saturday.

"We'll watch the sun rise," he said.

"Won't it be too cold?" I said.

"I'll bring blankets. I'll pick you up just before dawn."

"Will you buy me breakfast?" I said.

"Breakfast, lunch, and supper," he said.

"I'll ask my parents."

My father smiled when I told him. He lifted his coffee cup into the air. "To Sam," he said. "He's a real romantic, isn't he?"

"I guess he is," I said.

"If you want to go, it's fine with me." He turned toward my mother. "Lillian? What do you think?"

"It's not even summer yet," said my mother. "Won't you be cold?"

"That's what *I* said."

My father laughed. "Where's your spirit of adventure, ladies?" He poured himself some more coffee. "You're just like your mother," he said to me. "When I took her out camping, she brought her hair dryer with her." He pointed to his coffee cup. "She wanted coffee in bed, not around the campfire."

"So I can go?" I said.

"We trust you," my father said. "You can go." He had the last word. It was funny.

On Friday night, I washed my hair and put out my clothes, including a heavy sweater in case it was cold. I checked the newspaper for sunrise and set the alarm for an hour earlier. I got into bed. It was around nine-thirty.

Rachel came in, wearing a cotton nightie that made her look eight years old. "Are you sleeping already?" she said.

I patted the bed. "Not yet. Sit."

She sat next to me and leaned her head against the wall. I put a throw pillow behind her. We didn't talk.

Cara stuck her head inside my room. "Can I come in?" she said.

I patted the bed on the other side of me, and she climbed onto the mattress, settling herself against the wall with the rest of the throw pillows.

"Is everyone comfy?" I said, pulling the covers over all three of us.

Cara started laughing. "It reminds me of something," she said. "Like we did this before."

"Coming home from Grandma's at night," I said. "In our pajamas, in the back seat of the car."

"That's it!" said Cara. "And Mom gave us a blanket."

"I don't remember that," said Rachel.

"You were too young," I said.

We sat there peacefully, until I remembered my meeting at dawn.

"Does my hair look okay?" I said.

"That's right, tomorrow is the big day," said Cara. "You could wear a mop, and he'd like it."

"Where are you going?" said Rachel.

"To the beach. Sam and I are going to watch the sun rise." My father was right. It did sound romantic.

"Cheap date," said Cara, and I gave her a pinch even though I knew she was joking.

"Won't you be cold?" said Rachel, and that started me laughing until I saw the hurt look on her face, and I told her that Mom and I had said exactly the same thing.

"Dad says we have no spirit of adventure."

"Dad?" snorted Cara. "Dad is a nutcase altogether," but the minute she said it, she got pop-eyed, and the three of us started laughing until my mother came into the room and said, "What's going on here?"

"Nothing," said Rachel, her face all round and innocent.

My mother tilted her head to the side, and said, "Ahhhh." Her eyes were misty and she had this wistful expression on her face and she said, "My three girls," like we were in some old Hollywood movie.

"Ben!" she called. "Come and see."

We sat there, soft sculptures in bed, until my father came into the room. He put his arm around my mother, and they stood there looking at us. It seemed like hours that I was staring back at my parents' smiling faces, but it was probably only a matter of seconds.

I woke up with a start, to the sound of knocking.

"Honey," my father was saying, "I think you've overslept."

I grabbed the alarm clock and held it close to my face.

"Five o'clock! Oh, no!" I practically fell out of bed and struggled into my jeans. "I'm late!" I called to my father in the hallway. Sneakers, shirt, a comb through the hair, a swig of mouthwash, forget brushing.

I threw open my door and dashed downstairs into the living room, into the dining room, into the kitchen, where my father was making coffee.

"Is my pocketbook in here?" I said to him, and he pointed to a kitchen chair.

"Juice," he said, handing me a glass.

I took a swig of it and made a face. "Mouthwash and juice! Agh!" I looked at his face, his sweet father face making sure his daughter didn't go out into the world without something in her stomach, and said, "Delicious!"

Then I grabbed my pocketbook and ran back into the dining room, into the living room, and out the front door. The early-morning air was cool on my face, and there was Sam, sitting in his car drinking coffee from a thermos. He leaned across the seat, smiling, and opened the door for me. "I didn't want to wake everybody by ringing the doorbell," he whispered.

"I overslept," I whispered back.

"Put on your seat belt," he said as he turned on the ignition.

Sam pushed the stick into drive, which gave me just enough time to wave to my father, standing in the doorway. My father waved back.

JUDITH CASELEY

is the author and illustrator of over a dozen books for children. *Kisses*, her first young adult novel, was published in 1990 and was named an ALA Best Book for Young Adults. She writes about family and clinical depression from firsthand experience, as her father—a short story writer and novelist who gave her the inspiration to start her own literary career—has suffered from the illness. She lives in New York City with her husband and two children.